Greg's First Adventure in Time

C. M. Huddleston
2014

C. M. Huddleston
2015

Greg's First Adventure in Time

Published by:
Interpreting Time's Past, LLC
Crab Orchard, Kentucky

Cover by Interpreting Time's Past, LLC

ISBN: 978-0-692-31046-5

For Ethan and Ian
with all my love

Chapters

1
Excavations

Immediately after all this happened to me, I wanted to tell anyone, someone, everyone I knew or even didn't know, what had happened. Bad, bad idea, as I quickly learned. For as I began telling my tale, the listener thought weirdo, geek, or git. I mean, what happened to me turns out to have been one of those stories you read on the front of those tabloids—you know, the ones at the grocery checkout lane that you read while your mother is packing the groceries, using her debit card, and telling you for the four-millionth time that she will never bring you shopping with her again.

Now don't get me wrong. I am sort of a geek. I get good grades in school, not great, but good. I speak English and German (we once lived there), and I play a lot of computer games, like Minecraft. I like Minecraft. You can build things while axing to death Creepers and Zombies. I also like Halo and Guild Wars 2, when my friends or my Dad are playing. But, back to the geek part. I hang out with my Mom a lot, and well, she's different from most moms. Besides, my Dad's gone most of the time. I really can't explain him to you, if I did I think I'd have to kill you, or at least someone would.

Also, I talk. I talk to myself, to the computer, the dog, my hamster, to anyone around ... you get the idea. It started when I was three. I just started talking and didn't shut up. Mom and Dad, well at first they listened to me, then they just tuned me out. I think they pretended that I was talking to God as he was obviously the only one willing to listen after a few years of incessant one-sided conversations. Anyway, I have learned to be quiet when necessary—usually around strangers, and, well, girls.

Back to what happened, it definitely wasn't the type of thing one would expect a twelve-year-old boy to be telling. These days I only discuss my adventure with Mom, she believes me, and my computer (yes, I talk to the computer—told you that already). You see, I'm writing it all down in

2

Word Perfect (Mom hates Word), so in the future when someone else believes me, all the details will be there in living color, actually in blue on my computer screen, for all to read. I mean, it may be years before anyone except Mom, and maybe Dad, believes me. Now for my story. Perhaps I shouldn't call it a story, but an autobiographical sketch—not an autobiography—I'm only 12.

It all happened last summer. First you have to know, my Mom is an archaeologist. That's not *normal* for Moms. I mean all of my friends' moms are teachers, doctors, lawyers, work at the mall, or just stay at home. Not my mom. She studies ancient people by digging up the stuff they left behind in the dirt. Yes, yes, I know, *soil,* as she would say (she's a real stickler for using the correct name for things).

First, Mom got a degree in history and taught for a while. Then off she went, back to school, got a second, and then a third degree, and started living her *dream*. Right now she works at a small archaeological site called Cresaptown. It is on the edge of the Potomac River in Maryland, just across the river is West Virginia. Not that you need to know that. When the archaeologists finish their excavations, it will become a county ballpark. Imagine playing baseball on top of an ancient burial ground.

Don't you think that's weird? I do.

I personally found it hard to imagine people had lived on that land for thousands of years. We're talking prehistoric man! Indians! All I could see there was a bunch of junk, artifacts, things they left behind. It was just too much to imagine people walking around in deerskin clothes, hunting big game, raising families, and dying right there. I guess Mom's imagination is better than mine.

So, all of that is how I came to be digging a large hole in the middle of an Archaic Indian site in late August instead of swimming, fishing, riding my bike, getting in a few hours of *Minecraft* or *Halo,* or just plain goofing off. Personally, but don't tell anyone, Mom's dream isn't too bad. I mean we really do find lots of neat stuff. Oh, yeah, better tell you, archaeologists recognize four periods of prehistoric (that means before writing) man. Mom says the four periods are called Paleoindian, Archaic, Woodland, and Mississippian. They can actually recognize how long ago the people lived on a site simply by looking at a few artifacts. Weird.

My personal archaeologist, better known as Mom, works at the dig or "excavations" all summer and does research and analyzes her finds during the rest of the year. Now on this particular summer day, she was calling me her "assistant." Several screens, wooden boxes with heavy screen mesh bottoms, hung from tripods, you know, three-legged stands. Plus, Mom always has an abundance of shovels (square and round), root cutters, string, and other equipment for volunteers. Eleven ten-year-olds were visiting the site, to "learn the basics of archaeology." It was part of some kind of history camp. My job was to make sure they learned how to screen the soil and looked carefully for any artifacts.

We had been at it ALL morning. I mean those kids couldn't tell the difference between a piece of plastic lid someone had thrown from a car window and a piece of bone. All I heard all morning was, "Greg, what's this?" and "Greg, should we keep this?" and "Greg, he shook dirt all over my new tennis shoes!" MAN! No matter how many times we told them to wear old clothes, the girls still showed up looking like an ad out of *Seventeen*. Weird!

I was happy to see lunch time come, thinking I could stretch out beneath a tree with my sandwich and a Cherry Coke and hope all of the girls at the pool across the street had on small bikinis. I mean, I do notice girls, I just don't talk around them.

But it wasn't happening.

Right before lunch, Mom uncovered a *feature*. I guess I'd better explain that the top layer of soil is called the *plow zone*. That is the layer most people would call the topsoil. In most of the eastern United States, and especially in Maryland where Mom was working, the land has been farmed at some time. You see when the farmers plowed the land that top level, the plow zone, got all mixed up. That mixing caused the artifacts, the things the Indians left behind, like bones from food, projectile points (arrowheads to you novices), the pieces of stone from which they were made, and fragments of pottery—if they had pottery—to be move about. So we shoveled this layer off into the screens and sifted through it carefully for the artifacts.

Underneath this level is the subsoil. Archaeologists use trowels, a hand-held triangular steel blade with a wooden handle, to carefully scrape the top of the subsoil clean of all the plow zone soil. Mom can do this so neatly that the unit walls are perfectly straight, the corners are ninety degree angles, and the floor is even and smooth. She doesn't do this just to be neat, since occasionally in the subsoil, an archaeologist will find what is called a *feature*. That's what she's looking for—features.

Features are places where the prehistoric people carried out different tasks, like cooking, tool and pottery making, butchering animals, and even burying their dead. These tasks often leave a dark stain in the soil because of rotting organic material, or if it was a hearth, it may be red from burning or black from the ash. A feature can tell an archaeologist a lot about how the people of the area lived. As for me, it just meant that we, Mom and I, would WORK through lunch. I mean, no way was she going to let those ten-year-old jerks mess up her research.

Now understand, Mom has several trowels. She is particularly fond of the first one she ever bought. Over the years, she has sharpened it so many times that it is much smaller than when it was new. It's like a baby trowel, actually it is older, but you get my meaning. Anyway, she uses a fairly new one for most of her work, but always digs out her favorite for excavating features. She says it works better because it is smaller.

On this day, she had decided I should excavate the feature, claiming it would be "good experience" for me. Experience for what? Who needs that skill in their adult life? It really didn't look half as exciting as watching the girls at the pool, but I couldn't—WOULD NOT—explain that to Mom.

So I stripped off my old tee (maybe the girls would notice my buff—okay, skinny—body) and tennis shoes, so that the tread wouldn't leave a design in her nice clean unit floor, and got busy. The first bit was extremely boring, just a lot of small, I mean tiny, old bones that Mom said were probably rabbit. Then all of the excitement started. Well, it was exciting to me. Everyone else was oblivious.

As I carefully troweled away the dirt from the bones in order to expose them for a photograph (don't I sound professional), I uncovered a projectile point.

Now for all you readers that know nothing about archaeology, a projectile point is what most people call an arrowhead. But since bows and arrows were not all that widely used and spears were certainly more common back in prehistoric times, all archaeologists insist these stone tools be called *projectile points*. First off, this projectile point was just lying there—smack dab in the middle of those bones—unbroken and glittering in the sun. It was made of quartz, a stone which has lots of crystals to catch the sunlight and not found naturally in this area. Even though we were working under a canopy, the sun really made this one glitter. I should let you know, I had been talking all this time, just to myself, no big deal, no one listens.

"Hey! Come look at this point right in the middle of these bones."

Mom jumped.

"Greg, please don't address me by yelling 'Hey!' Especially when I am only a foot away," she corrected me instantly.

I keep forgetting that she is my mother not my best buddy, which is how she seems when we work together like this.

"Ahhhh, Mom, not now! Just crawl over here and take a look. I mean this is really neat."

I remember we discussed what a super fantastic photo it would make and then she told me to carefully lift the point out of the bones and wipe it clean so it would show up better in the shot. (She used the words "photograph more clearly.") Then I had to carefully place it back where I found it. I was being really careful. Those bones were old and crumbly, and I knew she would be upset if they were disturbed before she got her photo. I, on the other hand, had already captured the image with my phone when she wasn't looking. I could send it off later to Dad—where ever he was.

Dad and I keep in touch by phone. We are always sending photos of cool stuff back and forth. Some of these we do not share with Mom. But more on Dad later.

Anyway, I carefully fitted the end of her baby trowel under the edge of the point and gently lifted it from among the bones. As I stood up, trying not to drop the point or step on anything, ALL HELL BROKE LOOSE! Yes, I know I said Hell. If you keep reading you'll understand why.

Anyway, a huge brown rabbit flew through the air straight into Mom's neat excavation unit and landed in the plastic zip lock bag holding the artifacts. Mom screeched (she was startled not scared), and I jumped so high I hit the overhead canopy. It quickly started falling in around my head. My arm flew up, the projectile point and mom's trowel shot through the air and landed right on top of that poor frightened rabbit at the exact instant he had recovered his head from the artifact bag.

Now all of this takes much longer to tell than it took to happen, but the next few seconds seemed to take years. As I reached for the trowel and the point, the rabbit jumped sky high and all three landed on my hand.

Then my world changed.

Suddenly, I stood in the middle of a dappled green forest filled with huge oak, chestnut, and hickory trees on the edge of the river, the Potomac, I think. I held a scared, shaking rabbit, a trowel, and a projectile point. Only now the point was attached to a wooden shaft and deeply embedded in the bleeding rabbit—which was dying. The canopy, screens, tripods, the excavations, and even Mom had disappeared.

I was sure it was all a dream, like Dorothy in the Wizard of Oz (I kept thinking please don't let there be flying monkeys, I hate those monkeys!). That was it, I had hit my head and was unconscious, please just let me be unconscious. Unconscious, yeah, that's it, unconscious. Better than this being real.

Nope. Not unconscious. Not dreaming. Still awake.

As I stared, the rabbit stopped shaking and lay bleeding in my hand while only five feet away stood a small, darkly tanned boy dressed in these bizarre leather britches and holding another spear exactly like the one I was holding, except it didn't have a bloody rabbit attached. He kept his spear pointed right at me. Right at my heart. Nope, not a dream. *Definitely not a dream.*

At first, I just stood there, shaking. I was befuddled for sure. I mean, who does this happen to? Not me. At least it had never happened before. I soon figured out he wanted his rabbit. I sure as heck didn't want it. By the way, I wasn't talking—dumbstruck for the first time in my life.

Slowly, I pulled the spear point from the rabbit, a really gross, I mean really, really gross experience, and laid the rabbit on the ground. I held onto the trowel and the spear, for some unknown reason, and said, "Take it, it's yours," while pointing to the rabbit, which was now quite dead. The boy just stood there staring and pointing that huge spear at me. Never even blinked.

I thought about running. I am pretty good at running, but not much else as far as athletics. I'm tall for my age, a blue-eyed blonde, just like good ol' Dad. But something of a geek, I think I told you that already. I mean, what chance did I have against a spear throwing Indian! Yes, I knew he was an Indian, didn't know what period, but I should have from the type of projectile point. But no time to think about such details now.

It looked longer and sharper each time I looked at it, the spear that is. It was impossible not to look at it. I tried. But every time I decided to concentrate on his face instead of that spear point, my mind shouted "WHY IS HE POINTING THAT THING AT ME?" I wanted to cry "MOM." But if I was unconscious, and those girls in tiny bikinis had come over from the pool to see what

12

all the excitement was about, I didn't want to sound like some scared babbling crybaby. I was still hoping for unconscious. Much less scary than what was happening.

For what seemed like ages, we both stood there facing each other. He holding a spear pointed at me, and me holding a spear covered in blood and Mom's trowel, with a dead rabbit on the forest floor at my feet. We must have been quite a sight, since by now both of us were shaking. Finally, I decided to try offering him the rabbit again. After all, I was quite sure he had killed it. Besides, he looked hungry and more than a little threatening with that gigantic spear in his hand.

So, I carefully lifted the rabbit from the ground while keeping my eyes directly on his. My karate sensei always told us to keep your eyes on your opponent. The rabbit was still warm, but had stopped bleeding. I held it out in his direction and whispered, "Here it's yours."

It seemed strange that such tiny words could have overcome his fear so quickly. But he smiled, laid his spear on the ground, and took the rabbit, being very careful not to touch my hand. Then he grasped the small dark stone hung around his neck and spoke several words in a language I had never heard. Though the sounds were foreign, I instantly understood their meaning. How was that possible? I mean, I understood an ancient language! This was some freaky weird dream. Not real. Really, not real. Right? Couldn't be real, could it?

He said, "God of the Stone, thank you for this rabbit."

In my mind, I was thinking *now go away so I can wake up and get some sympathy from those girls.* But reality seemed to be right there in that forest with the dead rabbit and the quite real Indian.

"God of the Stone, you may keep my spear in exchange for the rabbit you have provided. Do you wish to share in my meal?"

I hesitantly answered in his language, searching my memory for the right words (again, really, really far out). "Are you speaking to me?" I don't know why I was speaking so properly, I think it was fear. Maybe I would just give up talking altogether—probably not.

"Yes, God of the Stone, since your rabbit is to be my meal and you have appeared before me, I offer you the best parts. After all, only the tales of my grandmother speak of you appearing to us to share in the bounty of the hunt. Her tales are of a time out of mind."

14

All of this he said while standing very still, with his hand clasped around the dark stone hanging against his chest. But he had lowered the spear.

"Yes, I'll share the rabbit with you, ah, but only if you cook it first."

"Grandmother says the God of the Stone likes a good joke, but I must use two hands to skin and cook the rabbit. Will you remain if I release my hold on your spirit or will you go, taking the rabbit with you?"

Now I wasn't sure exactly what he was talking about. I mean, was he holding my spirit in this dream? If, I said yes, would he release it so I could wake up? Why did he call me God of the Stone? How could I understand him? A million questions ran helter-skelter through my mind. At least they didn't spill out of my mouth. Besides, I didn't even know if I liked rabbit. Never had it before.

Out of desperation and hunger, (I hadn't finished my sandwich) I whispered, "Let's eat."

2
Lunch

He released the stone hanging around his neck, and I realized it was similar to some of the gorgets Mom and I had found at the site. Gorgets are smooth, carved, flat stone pendants that prehistoric men and women wore—a huge necklace, made out of rock. Weird, huh?

I didn't disappear or wake up. Darn.

The boy then pulled a sharp-looking stone knife from a small leather pouch hung over his shoulder and around his neck. Someone had hafted a finely chipped black chert knife to a small curved

16

piece of light-colored wood. Mom had said that chert, sometimes mistakenly called flint, was a local stone found at several quarries along the river.

He quickly began skinning and gutting the rabbit. Now I had thought pulling the spear from the rabbit was really sickening, but this totally wiped me out. So I stopped watching. I mean, in Minecraft, we can butcher meat, but there's no blood or guts. Guts stink. I mean really stink.

The Indian—I have to call him that because I didn't yet know his name—finished up the skinning and gutting process in a couple of minutes. Really, no more than three minutes! I could tell he had done this more than once.

Then he started a fire, again amazingly quick. Now in Cub Scouts, we had learned about twirling sticks to cause friction and start a fire. But this young boy simply pulled out some material which looked like dried moss, and two odd stones from his pack. By flicking the stones together, he created sparks in the moss, blowing gently to start a small flame. Quickly adding small sticks and old, dried leaves from the area around him, he soon started a small fire.

He seemed truly shocked when I began to gather small branches and even an old limb to add to the fire. Maybe the God of the Stone doesn't do manual labor. I broke the limb into several pieces, using my foot as leverage, and handed them to him. During all of this, he did not speak. Neither did I. I was terrified. I had no idea why he was quiet.

My growing terror increased with every minute. What was happening to me? I seemed to have some control over my body and actions. But, I didn't know how I got there—where *there* was—or how to get out of *there*.

My heart thumped in my chest as tears settled behind my eyes just waiting to flow. It seemed like a nightmare, only I honestly didn't think I was asleep or unconscious.

As he spitted the rabbit and began to cook it over the fire, I gathered together what little courage I possessed. Deciding to use a direct approach for getting some answers, I asked, "What's your name?"

He blurted out, "Hopelf, son of Cray of the People of the Long Valley with the Long Mountain."

What a name! He'd never be able to put all of that on one of those dumb computer test forms where you have to put a letter in each block, with a number 2 pencil. I decided just to call him Hopelf, (pronounced Hoe-pef) even if it was a strange name.

Now for more questions. "Where are we?"

"Does the God of the Stone not recognize the Long Valley with the Long Mountain?"

So much for that question. Try another approach. "What year is it?"

"The year after the Dry Year when the Mother Died. Of course, it has no name because we are not yet come to the first snow. The God of the Stone likes to ask funny questions. Grandmother has told many times of your deeds for the People. The stories often make us laugh. Now I know the laugh is in the God of the Stone, too," he replied while carefully turning the rabbit over the fire.

Strange, Hopelf also rambled from one sentence to another. He sounded somewhat like me.

Anyway, so much for the direct approach. "Hopelf, are your father Cray and your people nearby?" I asked, thinking an indirect approach might work better.

"Cray is my grandmother," he replied softly glancing up from the fire.

He began to look at me rather oddly and even a bit suspiciously. He seemed to think that I didn't seem quite right. Obviously, I needed to phrase my questions more carefully if I was going to get any answers. As my mind rushed ahead, I waited, not talking, trying to decide what to do next.

"As the God of the Stone seems to need to hear me speak, I will tell the story of the People of the Long Valley with the Long Mountain. I will tell the story while we eat."

He had spoken quietly again, still looking at me as though I were a mystery. Some mystery, more like science fiction!

"But first might the God of the Stone like to tell me why he has appeared? Am I to be chosen as one of your own?" he finished, speaking even more quietly than before. There seemed to be a tremble in his voice, as if he were scared. I know I was.

Abruptly, I realized everything had changed. Now I had to answer questions. I couldn't very well tell the truth now, could I? Besides, what was the truth? Had I really been transported through time? If so, how? How far back? Would I ever go home? The chances of finding a wizard and ruby slippers seemed very far out.

I recall how I closed my eyes, meditating to control my thoughts and emotions just like I had learned in karate, and wished that when I opened them I would be back in the hot sun digging holes, sweating, and thinking only of girls in teeny, tiny bikinis. No such luck.

I opened my eyes to find Hopelf patiently watching me. Think quickly, my mind whispered, "Make it good, or he will never believe you."

After a while, Hopelf began to cut chunks of the hot, juicy rabbit meat and place it in two tortoise shells he had retrieved from his pack, sprinkling what I assumed was salt on each. I had already noticed that the smell of the roasting meat made my mouth water and my stomach growl. I may have been terrified of my current situation, but it was lunch time. I was hungry.

Just as quickly and efficiently as he did everything else, Hopelf took some kind of skin pouch and filled it with water from a nearby stream. Mom had noticed the stream on her first visit to the site commenting in her journal that at one time it must have provided lots of clean, cold drinking water. I had only noticed how dirty it had been and how full of trash, no good for wading or fishing, just like the Potomac River. But as the water gurgled into the bag, it was sparkling and clear. I could see every pebble and rock in the bottom of the stream, just like looking through glass.

My mind raced through every possible scenario. Every minute my predicament proved more troublesome. My conclusion seemed to be that I had traveled through time to this long-ago era. If what I had learned from Mom and other archeologists was correct, the projectile point he had used meant I had traveled about 3,000 years into the past. I now stood in the period called *Archaic*, before bows and arrows, before pottery, sometime before A. D.

Yep, way back in B. C. Just like the comic strip. I was in the prehistoric days of North America. I didn't think it was weird. No not weird, just scary, extremely mind-blowing, terrifying in fact.

Pulling myself together, I turned back to watch Hopelf's actions. I hoped as he finished arranging the meal that the God of the Stone was not going to be asked to bless the food. I hated being asked to pray before strangers and always tried to get out of it at family and church gatherings. But it seems it wasn't necessary. He didn't even make me wash my hands before he handed me the bowl, offered the water bag, and began to eat.

The rabbit tasted hot and delicious, sort of a mix between chicken and pork, but it needed more salt. The water was still cold as I drank deeply from the bag, but my Cherry Coke would have been better. Hopelf had promised to tell the story of his people while we ate, yet it seemed he waited for an answer to his previous question first. I calmed my nerves and decided to play along—you know, go with the flow—hoping I could figure out this totally weird situation as time went by.

So I answered him, rather quietly for me, "I, Greg, God of the Stone, came here to visit with you, Hopelf. I am searching for a friend to help me with a large task and am hoping you are to be that friend."

I volunteered my name because I was tired of being called God of the Stone. I mean, *really*, I'm not a god. Besides it was awkward. Can you imagine trying to get someone's attention quickly and having to yell out "Hey, you, God of the Stone!"

Hopelf looked up sharply at the word Greg. As he spoke, I realized why. "The Grandmothers say the God of the Stone is named Tallilopka. In our legends, there is another named Greg, but that is a story we do not learn until we are old. Did you change your name or have we learned the wrong name since time out of mind?" he asked quizzically.

Brilliant thinking on my part, why hadn't I realized they probably had another name for the God of the Stone? Duh! My mind raced, Hopelf seemed even more suspicious. He actually backed away a bit. Really, did he think I planned to attack him? Did gods do that?

Finally, all of some boring story about the Navajos we had read last year in English class came flooding into my somewhat tormented brain. They had numerous names for each god. So I told him Greg was only one of my names along with Tallilopka. This seemed to quell his suspicions, but only somewhat. At any rate, he now began his story.

Listening proved easier than answering questions.

3
Hopelf's Story

Hopelf spoke in a way that reminded me of how Mom said legends had been passed from generation to generation by storytellers all over the world, especially by civilizations that did not have a written language. You know, prehistoric peoples. Hopelf spoke like he had memorized the story word for word. I guess you can do that when you hear a story over and over.

His story began at the very beginning, sort of once upon a time like, explaining creation along with the lifeways of the group he called the People. I don't know that I had wanted to know quite so much about his people, but it quickly became fascinating. I listened without speaking (not dumbstruck this time, just listening) not wanting to interrupt as he told the tale of the People of the Long Valley with the Long Mountain.

"Our People came to this valley during the time of the Mother of All, the time out of mind. The Mother of All had finished creating the world, placing the animals on the Earth in order so each would be prey and be preyed upon. She created the many plants. Those to give shelter, those to give food, and those to give life to her creatures. She formed the People. She gave them and only them ideas.

"In exchange for the ideas, she took away their natural ability to hunt for food. They were prey. There was no animal they could kill, because they had not the strength, nor the skills. They did not know which plants to eat. She wanted them to use their ideas to feed themselves. But winter came. Her People were starving. So she used the last of her energy to create Tallilopka, her son. The God of the Stone.

"Her last words told Tallilopka to lead her People in search of food. The Mother of All gave her being to create the Earth. She became the Earth. She is here in the sky, in the plants, the animals, the rocks, the water, even the People. She is our Mother.

"We, the People, came to be during the winter, and so our years are named and numbered from winter to winter. We followed the God of the Stone. He led us to the Long Valley with the Long Mountain. Here we remained for it is our home, given to us from the Mother through her son. Tallilopka taught us. The People learned how the stone could make tools. The tools could be used to hunt and shelter the people. We came to hunt mammoths. The God of the Stone led us. All of the People, men and women alike, made tools. He taught us all.

"We all hunted, as the mammoths were large. It took many to make a kill by crowding and forcing the huge beasts into the swamps and bogs where they were immobilized and speared.

"Skinning the animal created another day's work. We used every part of the mammoth leaving nothing to waste, eating what we could fresh, then drying the leftover meat for winter. Tallilopka led us in the hunts, showing us how to use ideas to create clothing, shelters, and prosperity. We survived the winter. Tallilopka appeared less and less often. We needed him less and less. With the Spring, he left on a long journey promising to return when we again had need of his teaching, his ideas. By now, we could use the ideas that the Mother of All had given each of us.

"The People prospered. Children were born. The People spent happy days laughing. So was the Year the Mother of All Gave the People Ideas. That was the first year.

"Many, many years passed and during the time out of mind, the People continued to prosper. As the People became numerous, the families split. We learned it was easier to feed and shelter smaller groups. Each followed the Grandmother, the oldest mother of all amongst the different groups of People. It was she who gave each year a name.

"The People met once a year, usually during the early summer, at the beginning of the river as we still do today. Each family group has its own Grandmother who leads the family in all matters. In this way, we honored the Mother of All.

"Those times are out of mind with only the years when Tallilopka returned being remembered by name. The years were as many as the fish in the streams when the People hunted mammoths and prospered. Tallilopka returned when the mammoths left. Again we were hungry. Our ideas could not overcome the hunger. The winters of those years turned extremely cold, the ice came from the mountains, the summers never came. Our old and our young perished. The People despaired.

"Many, many more years passed. The People survived. Then the winters became more mild. Each summer was hotter and hotter as though the sun was creeping up on the Earth. The grasslands became deserts. The forest shrank. Different trees and plants grew. The old ones on which we had come to depend disappeared. Many swamps and bogs dried up as did many lakes and rivers. Mother of All changed her face.

"With each passing year, the other large game, the giant bison, the large cats, came no more. Even the giant beaver no longer swam in our rivers. The short-faced bear was no longer in the forest waiting to kill. The People had to kill smaller animals, but the tools and hunting techniques were not as effective as they had been with the mammoth. The People knew only the old ways.

"Tallilopka returned. He taught us new tools. We had to learn new ways to chip the stone, to hunt the animals. It was during this time when the women learned more about the plants. The women hunted less. But it was a Grandmother who used her ideas to teach us to fish.

"Tallilopka stayed until we had learned to make new types of shelter and clothing. We learned to weave plants and to build homes of sticks and mud and hides. Tallilopka stayed only until our ideas advanced what he had started. Then he proceeded on his journey. The Grandmothers say he travels today teaching his people as the Mother of All instructed him to do.

"Today, my family, the family called Cray for our Grandmother, lives yet in the Valley. We move from hunting camp to hunting camp in the Valley during the summer. We fish in the streams and in the Great River of the Valley. As we travel, we visit the places of plants. We gather nuts and grains for the winter.

"In the winter, we return to the Long Mountain to our shelter of rock where we number the cold days with nights of storytelling and ceremonies for the old and new year. We also learn the stories of the time out of mind so the Mother of All will not be forgotten and will remember her People. The Grandmother tells the tales of Tallilopka so his name and deeds will be remembered. There are many tales of his visits to our People and to the distant People of the Mother of All. We repeat them to the Grandmother so that she knows we have learned them correctly.

"So are the years and days of the People of the Mother of All since the time out of mind."

Wow!

4
Fishing

I could tell Hopelf had learned the story his Grandmother taught him very well. He told the story without pausing except to eat small bites of the rabbit and once to drink from the water bag. I finished the meal and found myself to be quite relaxed, like years ago when my mother had read me a nap time story every day after lunch. My anxieties melted away.

I wanted to hear and learn more about his people and the Mother of All. I had so many questions roaming about in my brain. Like how did I understand his language so well? How many gods did they have? How did I get here? I especially wanted to hear more about these deeds of Tallilopka, for whom Hopelf had mistaken me. But it was not to be. I was not to get answers so quickly.

Now, I should have been ready for anything after the events that had already occurred that day. But Hopelf's next suggestion took me totally by surprise.

"Would Greg like to swim and catch fish with me?" he asked.

My first thought was SWIM in the POTOMAC, that dirty, nasty, polluted river of waste? No way Jose! Then I remembered how clean the stream had been. The river might be the same. I had to remind myself that I was in "a time out of mind" whatever that meant.

We walked silently toward the river. At least it was in the same place! The forest teemed with wildlife. Even on the short walk we saw gray squirrels, a red fox, several busy chipmunks that showed little or no fear, and even the five-toe, five-claw tracks of a rather large black bear. Dad taught me how to recognize animal tracks. Comes in handy at times like these.

As we approached the river, a small herd of white-tailed deer scattered at our approach. Two small speckled fawns lay partially hidden in the tall grass near the trail. I suspected their mother had not moved very far away. Hopelf ignored all of the animals. I, on the other hand, wondered at the abundance.

We swam for several minutes, in the buff. You know, skinny dipping. No one was around to see. When we had arrived at the river's bank, Hopelf had quickly stripped off everything but his gorget. I did the same leaving only the gold chain with the ring my father had given me hanging around my neck. The water was cool and sparkling with a clear green color because of the many trees along the banks providing a deep shade.

A foot-worn dirt path followed close by on both banks leading my eyes downstream to a small clearing. Hopelf explained that another family group camped in that area almost every fall. They used the clearing for processing and drying the meat to be stored for the winter. I had already filed this away to tell Mom so she could check it out for artifacts, when I realized the area was now covered by houses. She would have been ecstatic. Oh, well.

After swimming, splashing, and chasing a dappled brown snapping turtle near the grassy shore for a while, Hopelf climbed the bank and returned with a fiber net and a basket. Oh, yeah, he said swimming and *fishing*.

I wasn't sure how this was going to work, but I didn't want to seem dumb—for a god, that is. I knew I had already asked way, way too many questions, for Hopelf not to be suspicious. Quietly, Hopelf moved across the river, motioning for me to be quiet and to follow him. We approached an area where a small stream emptied into the river.

I soon discovered that by placing the net at the mouth of the small stream we could catch fish as they swam both into and out of the river. It took patience, since it was necessary to be very still while holding the net. Once the fish were captured, a lot of yelling and laughing went into grabbing them and throwing them into the basket on shore. Time after time, either Hopelf, a fish, or I became so entangled in the net that the laughter seemed as loud as the splashing, often with our catch being able to escape more quickly than ourselves.

I had never had this much fun fishing with my father. His way is much too quiet. When the basket was full, Hopelf dumped it onto a grassy area and threw the smaller fish back into the green river. With each toss he yelled, "I'll catch you again when both of us have grown." He saved only four large bass—I think they were bass, not being an expert on prehistoric fish—which he returned to the basket. By attaching a lid with some kind of long cord and tying the end of the cord onto a small branch, he was able to slip the fish back into the water. Now they would live until we were ready to skin them. Over the noise of the fish catching frenzy, Hopelf had informed me they were to be our next meal.

Afterward, we swam for a while to cool off. Actually, I think we were "goofing off." Hopelf laughed about the fishing for it seems he could do it better without my help. I was not surprised by his insistence that even the girls and old women were better fishermen than me.

He taught me how to find freshwater mussels and snails by feeling the soft sandy bottom with our feet and then diving down to pry the mussel from the sand with our fingers. Bringing them to the surface, we tossed them ashore in a neat pile.

Finally, we raced across the slowly moving water from shore to shore before climbing out and resting stark naked on a section of grassy bank. It was then I realized I had made a friend.

Don't get me wrong. I have lots of friends. Well, only two actually. Now three.

Sometime later we walked naked back to the camp fire to dress. I noticed Hopelf stared oddly at my buttons. See, those particular cutoffs had a button fly instead of a zipper which I'm pretty sure he would have found really perplexing. He had looked sharply at the trowel when he didn't know I was watching, as if it were a larger mystery than the sudden appearance of the God of the Stone. But explaining metal to a prehistoric Indian boy was something I didn't even want to attempt. I mean really, explaining the idea of smelting ore—I learned that in Minecraft when I was five—would just blow his mind. So, I just remained mute.

I noticed his britches were of soft leather and did not actually fasten but simply lapped over to be held in place by another of those strange cords. He reached into his bag and pulled out leather shoe-like things which were not at all like the moccasins I have seen on TV Indians or even in museums. They pulled up over the ankle and most of the way to the knee and appeared to be a continuous piece of leather held in place by a long strip of soft, almost white rawhide wrapped from the heel upwards. His seemed to have molded in place to his feet. His actions in putting them on showed years of experience. I guess it's like tying shoes, once you learn, you can do it quickly without thinking.

As I had removed my sneakers before I

journeyed to that place, I had no shoes. Hopelf noticed my problem. From his seemingly bottomless leather pouch, he produced another pair and handed them to me saying, "Cray always insists I bring two pairs when I travel on the Journey Alone to Being a Man."

"How long does your journey last?"

"This is the third summer of my Journey Alone. This fall at the Killing of the Last Bison, I take Tlin, daughter of Orna, as my wife," he replied proudly.

"You're getting married?" I bellowed in complete shock. I mean Hopelf looked younger than me, and I had no thoughts of marriage. I only looked at girls. I couldn't even date. I mean, I didn't even talk to girls.

Hopelf eagerly explained, "I am of the age to marry as I have already fulfilled the first two summers of living alone and caring for myself to prove I am a man. At the end of two summers, I returned to my family with dried meat, skins, firestones, berries, even fresh fish to prove I can provide for a wife. Tlin lived with my family during those two summers, just like this year. She proves her womanhood by helping care for the children of the group. She shows the elders she is able to build a home for us."

While I stood stunned, listening, Hopelf explained that after the marriage, the Grandmothers, Cray and Orna would decide which of the large groups would become family to the new couple. It always depended on which group needed a young new couple to produce children and provide for the elders. He wasn't bragging about all this, just telling it like it was no big deal. I guess it wasn't to him.

Hopelf believed they would become Tlin and Hopelf of the Cray because his brother had no children after many years of marriage. The family needed the young members to assure its prosperity. Tlin would become of the Cray, and if she was ever the oldest mother of the group, her name would be changed to Cray. She would be the leader.

Finally, my feet laced into the leather boots, I realized they fit perfectly, since they stretched. The bottom contained a soft padding which I soon discovered provided a cushion over sharp stones and even small thorns. Hopelf repacked his knapsack, wrapping the remaining rabbit meat (the large rabbit had provided too much meat for one meal) and the fresh mussels in separate pieces of leather. We put out the campfire with the water from the drinking bag and being boys, helped it along, if you know what I mean.

It seems that during his summers alone

Hopelf would establish a small camp for himself. There, he could store food and supplies and also those things which he was collecting to take to the group with the coming of autumn. That's where we were headed.

I carried Mom's trowel, the spear, and the fish basket and net. Hopelf remained reluctant to let me do any of the labor. But I insisted. Being a god had its advantages.

His camp sat nearby, in a very small clearing only a few yards from the bank of the stream on the edge of Mom's site. I realized now he had earlier retrieved the basket and net for fishing from here. Everything had its place. He kept it really neat, not at all like my room at home. I'm somewhat of a slob. After returning the fish basket to the small stream, Hopelf put the net, mussels, and rabbit meat away in a flash.

I could tell the day's adventures might not be over, because he continued to wear the knapsack around his neck and picked up yet another spear in addition to the one he already carried. He offered me an additional spear and for some strange reason I took it. I pushed the point of the trowel into my back pocket in order to be able to carry it without tying up the use of my hands. The spear shafts were lightweight and flexible. I knew that would give the spears greater strength so they would not break upon impact—see Mom, I have been listening all these years. Someone had knapped the points out of the same dark chert as his knife, very unlike the quartz one which had started this entire adventure.

"Now we will gather berries," he proclaimed while producing two small baskets. "We must speak loudly along the trail as the bears love the berries, and I don't have need for another skin."

Bears! Here? Really, with everything else, now I have to worry about bears?

I didn't have a use for even one bear skin, so I shouted, really shouted, everything I said. Hopelf found this extremely funny and insisted it would make a great story for the winter nights. I can just imagine now how Hopelf's story would make me seem foolishly afraid of the bears while carrying two spears. To tell the truth I had no desire to meet up with a bear while carrying only a spear, okay two spears. I was sure I couldn't hit even the broad side of a bear with one of those things.

We saw only a black snake along the path and some large deer at the edge of the stream, which bounded off through the trees as we approached. Hopelf claimed it was because of all the noise I was making. The berry bushes were covered with sweet, ripe blackberries so sticky with sugar that each of us was soon covered with reddish black syrup. No bears came to eat, us or the berries, but recent tracks in the path's soft soil made me realize they had visited the site since the last rain.

We filled both baskets with berries and, of course, our stomachs. Hey, I was hungry after all that swimming and fishing. Actually, I'm always hungry. That's why Mom hates taking me to the grocery.

5
First Night

Mom always says time flies when you're having fun. That day proved no different. By the time we returned to Hopelf's hunting camp, the sun had begun to set behind Dans Mountain, its current geographical name. We washed in the stream upon our arrival, and again I watched as Hopelf built a fire and proceeded to roast the fish and mussels we had caught earlier. The reality of all that had happened hit me as the darkness spread as the setting sun dropped rapidly behind the mountain.

The day's humid heat dropped slowly as the greens of the surrounding forest turned to grays and black. I wasn't wearing a watch, but knew it to be around nine o'clock as we began to feast on the fish.

With the darkness came fear. No, I'm not afraid of the dark, that was the least of my worries. Hopelf had accepted me as the God of the Stone from the instance of my first appearance, but the sudden changes in time and place proved too frightening for me to comprehend or accept. I excused myself into the surrounding darkness following a path I now knew, only faintly visible in the moonlight, and returned to the spot of my time travel.

I guess I expected to walk back into my time, find Mom, and go home. Nothing happened. Nada. Nothing at all.

The tears that had threatened to flow earlier returned with the force of a steep mountain waterfall. I sat huddled under a spreading chestnut canopy, its trunk rough against my back, weary head on my knees, with only the moon and the Mother of All's creatures to hear my sobs. I'm not sure how long I remained there alone. I must have slept some.

Later upon waking to a bright full moon overhead, I found myself to be quite cold. I returned through the damp chill to Hopelf's camp and found him asleep, covered with a fur blanket under a lean-to of branches. Spread nearby was another blanket,

I guess he thought I might return. Sleep came as quickly as the warmth.

The squalls, chirps, and songs of dawn's bird chorus and early-rising energetic squirrels woke me soon after sunrise. The night's chilly air persisted, and the ground lay damp with dew. I arose quietly and gathered more sticks for the fire. It endured only as red embers.

Hopelf lay awake under his hide blanket, but pretended otherwise. With the first blaze of the fire, he seemed to accept my presence and rose to begin breakfast. More berries, cold rabbit meat, and water filled our stomachs. Conversation started weakly, because I didn't ask any questions, being afraid I would also have to answer any that might be asked of me.

As the rabbit meat disappeared, Hopelf suggested a plan for the day. We were to go hunting. Summer's end quickly approached, and Hopelf desired one more moose hide for his wedding gift to Tlin. He wanted it to be fairly fresh upon his return so Tlin could tan it with ease. He explained that some moose lived higher in the hills at an upland bog away from the river, making it necessary for the hunt to be an overnight journey.

This prospect of traveling so far from familiar turf might have frightened me if it had not been for the dream. I awakened with a feeling of relief and something that might even be called courage. For during the peaceful, warm part of the night as I slept beneath the fur of some strange animal, I dreamed of telling my mother my adventure. She seemed so close, so real. In the dream, as I spoke, she held the projectile point which had started this whole strange affair.

More important, she believed me. With the dawn, her presence had remained. Somehow I knew my time in this dimension would end. Dreams can be powerful things, and this one gave me the courage to face the days ahead.

Besides, what else could I do?

6
Moose Hunt

Hopelf carefully packed various supplies into two furry-skinned knapsacks. I think they might have been beaver pelts. In each bag he placed firestones, moss, extra projectile points, and two lightweight hides that reminded me of summer weight blankets. He donned a shirt of soft tan leather and handed me one also. It fit a little tight, but by loosening the ties we made it work. I added Mom's trowel to the bag he handed me and picked up my two spears as we left the camp. Hopelf doused the fire and covered his belongings and stores of supplies.

"Won't someone steal them?" I asked as we slipped into the forest.

Hopelf gave me another of those questioning looks as he answered, "Why should anyone steal from me when the Mother of All has provided such abundance for the taking?" He sure had a way of making me feel stupid.

We walked uphill almost from the beginning, sometimes following a stream that tumbled down the mountain side in a series of small waterfalls. At other times, a well-worn path led our steps. Mostly we walked in single file, me following him as the narrow path wound through trees, briars, and brush.

Rock outcroppings occurred more and more frequently as we climbed. Large limestone standing stones covered in petroglyphs, carved rock images pecked and scratched into the rock's surface, occurred frequently. Some appeared to be animals. Others to be men and women. Others looked more like a language. Hopelf told me they were old. He didn't know what they meant, only that his people once used the symbols to communicate with other people traveling through the area.

Once during our walk, I saw in the distance, smoke from a camp fire. Hopelf explained that it marked the camp of another boy on the Journey Alone. He knew of five others in the area, but they avoided contact except in times of illness or injury. Of the five, only Hopelf was in his third summer, the others were just beginning their time alone. He had not talked with any of the boys during that summer. Can you imagine going a whole summer and talking to no one?

He told the story of finding it necessary to return one boy to the family camp at the far end of the Valley during a previous summer. The boy had met with a wild boar during the days before and had wandered into Hopelf's camp sick from fever, his leg badly infected. I asked Hopelf if the boy had recovered.

His reply was soft and full of regret, "No, the Mother of All returned my mother's sister's son to her heart. He is no more with us, but has returned to the East." Their idea of what I assumed to be some kind of heaven seemed to give him comfort.

When Mom had excavated several burials at her site, we had discussed the age of each individual. Later, other archeologists, called anthropological pathologists, would examine each skeleton to determine sex, age, diet, and cause of death, if possible. Then the remains would be reburied in an area set aside by the State of Maryland for prehistoric burials. It's a secret location, known to only a few archaeologists and some Native American tribal leaders.

With little realization, I had watched Mom work with her baby trowel, a soft paint brush, and some soft bone tools carefully exposing and excavating each skeleton. These skeletons had held no sense of being for me. Yet as I saw the flash of grief Hopelf felt in losing his cousin, I could imagine these families that had existed so many years before. Hopelf's story told me of their joys and sorrows, their longings and accomplishments. He made them real, alive even, and I was now a part of their lives. Somehow I didn't think my life would ever be the same.

Dans Mountain rises steeply from the Potomac River valley floor. So, we walked on uphill for the better part of the morning along a trail often used by animals as well as man through the green and black of the dark forested mountain. We drank water from cold springs and watched deer, elk, and small game in some of the numerous clearings we passed. Hopelf speared a squirrel at one spring, providing us with food for the evening. We ate berries and chewed on dried meat for lunch.

Climbing almost to the top of Dans Mountain and then across a small saddle to an adjoining peak, we walked, a long, hard, hot walk. Late in the afternoon, just as I thought I would drop from sheer exhaustion, Hopelf heard a bellow on the wind and announced that moose were nearby. I hadn't heard even a whisper, but then I had been too busy wondering if it was possible to die from sore feet. I sure wanted my Nikes.

In a small clearing on the edge of the flat mountain peak, we quickly set up camp and left our extra gear under the lean-to we constructed from fallen logs, sticks, and cedar branches. Hopelf insisted rain would fall before morning making building a lean-to a necessity. Carrying only our spears, we ducked into the forest cover and approached a nearby stream, its banks covered in reeds and red elderberry. We were in search of moose. The area seemed to be some kind of upland bog.

Mom and I had visited an upland peat bog in nearby Garrett County to check out a chert quarry. This area looked very similar, and I recognized some rare species such as cottongrass and creeping snowberry. I watched for the elusive northern water shrew and the black bears the ranger said were known to inhabit the area. I didn't see either.

Meanwhile, Hopelf scurried up a giant chestnut and scouted around. He gestured for me to follow, and I did so quietly and quickly. I have always been good at climbing trees. But not climbing down, that's how I broke my arm when I was five, falling that is. Seems I'm not good at falling either.

"See, there, in the clearing," he said pointing to the west, into the sun, directly at the edge of a marshy looking area.

I stared amazed at five large male moose, or at least what I thought were males, chewing at the tall grasses or eating the small green leaves from low hanging branches along the edge of the clearing. One was moving his rack back and forth against a tree. Bark flew in all directions. They even ate the bark.

"We will kill our moose tomorrow morning if Greg, the God of the Stone, is willing."

I am still not sure if it was a question or a statement, but I just nodded my head up and down, while wondering how we could possibly kill such a large animal with only a spear. He must have sensed my question, my doubt. Really, two young boys take on one of those seven-foot-tall monsters. Are moose dangerous? Can they run fast? Will they trample a person? Where was Google when I needed it most?

Hopelf left the tree and silently circled the clearing, scrutinizing the ground as he went. Before long, he spotted three trails leading to and from the clearing. Using a vine, he tied strips of dyed red leather across one trail just at the edge of the trees. The moose, spooked for a moment by the movement of the strips, moved slightly away, before warily returning to their grazing.

As we circled wide to the other two trails, Hopelf explained, "We will close off two of the trails with strips to stir in the wind and then one of us will chase the moose down the other trail and under the trees. They will run right beneath the strong hunter whose spear will be sharp and true. Greg will understand when I insist upon making the kill as it is to be my wedding gift to Tlin."

Being relieved at not being called upon to spear a moose, I quickly agreed, but upon further thought, I wondered how easy chasing five large male moose down a forest trail would be. Two of those fellows had the largest racks I have ever seen. Too bad Tlin would not be happy with a ring for her finger instead.

Oh yeah, no metal.

We returned to our new camp and set about doing, well, camp things. You know, fire building, cooking, goofing off, etc. With little warning, the rain came crashing down through the trees followed by the first crack of thunder. Lightening lit the summer's dusky sky as gray clouds pushed down toward the valley below us. The fire, only just then hot enough for roasting our squirrel, quickly turned to soggy gray ashes. Hopelf and I huddled underneath the lean-to and stayed relatively dry. We had nothing to do, but wait. I slept.

I awoke to a dark star-studded sky visible through the trees surrounding our little camp and the great smell of squirrel roasting. Somewhere Hopelf had found dry wood. As he tended the browning meat, I went to a nearby spring for water. A large barn owl scooped down capturing a vole at the spring just as I arrived. It felt just like living a Nature Channel program.

We hungrily feasted on the freshly cooked meat and some type of wild apple Hopelf had picked during the day. Hopelf, who had seemed preoccupied during the evening, finally summoned up the courage to talk with me about what was bothering him.

"Why is Greg the God of the Stone so much like the People instead of the God from the stories of the time out of mind?" he asked with quiet hesitation.

I wanted to tell him the truth, really I did, but I had long since realized that his environment had not provided him with the means to understand. It wasn't that he was stupid or unintelligent, it was just that he had no background with which to comprehend the complexity of the situation. At least that's what I told myself.

So I lied.

"Hopelf, I came in this form because it best suited my needs. By appearing as a boy like yourself, I can learn how to help your people when you next have need of my ideas," I said, hoping he would buy the lie. I'm not very good at lying, Mom says my eyes twinkle when I do.

This seemed to ease his mind, because he next suggested that we eat, then sleep, in preparation for the coming day and its hunt. So we shook the few raindrops that had slipped between the branches of the lean-to off our hide blankets, and settled in for the night. I slept like a rock and on a rock. It left a bruise.

Morning brought sore muscles like I had never known. My feet felt like bruised, beaten masses of raw flesh. I knew what raw flesh looked like; I saw it yesterday, first rabbit and then squirrel. I could barely stand as I hobbled my way into the trees to heed the call of nature, so to speak. Crawling back into the lean-to, I removed the leather boots and examined my aching feet.

Hopelf, who had been fetching fresh water, caught me doing this and laughed. "Greg should have flown on the wind to reach the mountain for it seems he is not accustomed to walking."

"I wanted to experience your life, remember?" I growled back. This made him laugh even louder, but he wrapped my feet in cold leather strips he first soaked in the spring water, easing the ache. By the time we had finished a breakfast of more strange fruit and nuts and cold squirrel, I found I could pull on the leather boots to which he had added fresh padding and walk without limping. Well, almost without limping.

Hunt time had arrived. Oh, boy! (In case you didn't know, *that* was sarcastic, but I don't know how to write sarcasm.)

Nature films will never again look real to me. Moose hunting with rifles or even modern bows and arrows cannot compare to the thrill of the prehistoric hunt, a quick, bloody kill with man (actually boys) using brains over the brawn of several huge moose. At least I hoped that's how it would happen.

As I approached the clearing, three moose began to rise from the wet grass beds where they had spent the evening chewing their cud. Moose are ruminants, like cows. I learned that in biology.

Hopelf tied several strips of the red leather around my arms, showing me how to flap them up and down creating the effect of a large, noisy bird charging across the meadow toward the still (I hoped) drowsy beasts. At least that seemed to be the theory. I moved silently around the bog approaching the moose from one of the trails we had flagged the evening before. Hopelf, meantime, disappeared down the trail not marked with flagging. He needed to get into position for the kill.

As I walked, I realized what a sight I must be. Blue jean cutoffs, leather moccasins, hide shirt, bed head, dirty face, scratches, insect bites, carrying a large spear and limping slightly. We had also tied long strips of leather and feathers along the length of the spear so that when I waved it, it would seem alive. Again, that was the theory. I was not sure if I wanted to test the theory.

Hopelf explained that moose are easily startled by noise and unusual activity. He also said when a moose licks his lips he is about to charge. How could I watch their lips while running?

I think Hopelf failed to realize my need to understand all of the variables. After all, I was the one testing the theory. Too late now.

I snuck up on the moose from behind. Readied

myself both mentally and physically, and then waited. I listened carefully for the call of a certain bird, the saw-whet owl Hopelf had demonstrated over and over until I could recognize it. The waiting stretched on as I crouched in the reeds beside a small stream running through the bog.

I listened. I waited and waited and waited. I knelt. Crouching can be tiresome after a while.

A snake crawled slowly down a bank and entered the water, and all the while mosquitoes breakfasted on my blood. I didn't dare slap them away. Some buzzed my ears as others latched onto any available flesh. I watched the snake slithered closer and closer, then disappear into the reeds. It was mostly brown. Was that bad? Good? I needed a book on snakes.

Just then, I heard the call. A high pitched "too-too-too" repeated over and over.

It instantly occurred to me that Hopelf had not explained what I was to yell. "Shoo moosey, moosey" popped into my brain and sounded the most reasonable at the time. As instructed, I opened my mouth and yelled with all my might. Screaming, I flapped my way across the small stream, through the reeds where the snake had swam, and into the grassy clearing. I waved my spear, shouting even louder. At first the moose seemed to circle in confusion. Were they licking their lips? Who could look at their lips when they ran so fast, barreling over anything in their way? Reeds, mud, and debris flew from their hooves. Water splashed, birds took to the air, and squirrels chattered in alarm!

"Shoo moosey, moosey" rang again and again through the air.

More mud, peat moss, and water flew into the air in all directions. Branches fell from small bushes and trees. They separated and then rejoined in a kind of dance—the moose that is. Confusion reigned. It grew as they moved first closer to me, and then one I had not noticed earlier, moved directly toward me, swerving to the left and crashing into the stream just feet from my position. In the beginning of all this, I had observed only three moose. Now I realized there were four. WERE THEY MULTIPLYING?

I yelled louder, "Shoo moosey, moosey" and waved the spear over my head, and then stood stock still.

Bear. Big black bear. Yep, most assuredly a bear. There are no grizzly bears in Maryland right?

This made the whole confusing melee of running moose, swimming snake, crazy boy, and calling owl even more deranged and berserk. This had to stop. Why a bear? Where did the bear come from? Even more important, where was he going?

I didn't know if I should run, yell for help, freeze, play dead, or just cry.

The bear took charge. He, or she, bellowed, stood upright, did a little run in my direction, stopped looked around, and then ambled off into the trees on the far edge of the clearing. His backside wobbling to and fro as he picked up speed.

Two moose skedaddled off down the path where Hopelf hid. Another hustled off in the opposite direction from the bear, crashing between trees and bushes in his frightened flight. The final one caught his rack in some briars and bushes. That flat part of his rack threw water and foliage into the air creating a waterfall of debris. For just a moment, he set to bellowing and grunting an awful racket. Then, his thrashing head tore loose from the briars, and he resumed his headlong flight, briars and brambles trailing from his rack back across his rump. He looked even stranger than I did. I almost laughed.

Or I would have if the snake had not crawled across my foot at that very moment in time.

Rapidly, I pursued the two that had chosen the path. I could say calmly pursued, but that would be a downright lie. I pursued them still yelling "shoo moosey, moosey" down the path toward Hopelf simply because it seemed the path of least resistance. Also, the bear had not gone that direction. Discretion is the better part of valor. I learned that from Dad.

I arrived at Hopelf's hiding place in time to see the second moose crash to the ground partially on top of the first, both being pierced by Hopelf's spears. Quite dead, actually the second still twitched in death's throes. I always wanted to use that line. Read it in some book.

Hopelf scrambled from the tree while letting out a mighty yell of victory. But as with each kill before, he took the time to grasp his gorget and thank the God of the Stone for the kill. He was looking straight at me. It's cool to have such power (more sarcasm, in case you didn't catch that).

I sank to the ground right then and there and thanked God for not letting the moose run me down, or the bear eat me, or the snake bite me. I had a lot to be thankful for.

Sometime later I told Hopelf how impressed by his skill I was. Talking over the kill, I found out that Hopelf could see the clearing from his tree branch perch. He described the events of the last few minutes in great detail, laughing so hard he could barely stand upright. When Hopelf swore that it was my magical incantation that caused the bear to bellow and run off and both moose to follow the path allowing for the double kill, I realized that "shoo moosey, moosey" would go down in the tales of the People,

Boy was I embarrassed.

7
Hiding

It was still early in the morning. Already the hunt was over. Two boys, two dead moose. What an enormous problem. Well actually two of them. Under no circumstances could two boys carry those massive hides plus all that meat down that mountain. Hopelf also claimed some of the antler tines for chipping stone tools and numerous other parts for various purposes I didn't quite understand. I knew the path was too steep and rough for a travois to be of any use. I couldn't fathom how to solve this one. Tallilopka wasn't much on new ideas that morning.

Hopelf remained overjoyed at the kill, but also felt bad about wasting so much meat. He removed his spears from the beasts and searched his knapsack for the sharp stone knives necessary for the butchering process. He handed me one. I had watched during the previous day as he had butchered the squirrel, no longer feeling sick at such sights—well, not throwing-up sick. But I had no idea how to butcher a moose.

Hopelf slit the throat of each moose causing the blood to flow from the bodies making large dark puddles on the surrounding dirt. Then he sat and stared, looking very dejected. Hopelf did not seem to notice my hesitation as he now had yet another worry to add to his first. The second moose had fallen practically on top of the first, making it essential to separate them.

Pulling with all of our might, we first tried brute strength. That didn't work. Neither of us actually being a brute.

I suggested using one of the long vines as a pulley, so, we tied it to the antlers and looped it around a tree to give us extra pulling power. This was actually successful for a moment before the vine broke sending us flying backwards into a briar bush. We extricated ourselves and spent the better part of the next hour pulling thorns from each other's backside. Both of us proved smart enough not to try that trick again.

Our problems continued to lay there bleeding on the ground. Why can't things be as simple as they are in the movies? We were sitting despondently beside the two dead moose, when I first heard the voices of men nearby. Hopelf heard them at the same time and quickly climbed the tree to scout for their location. It took him several moments to spot the small hunting party through the thick green forest. When he did, his mood changed to one of elation. He knew them well, since some were of Oma's family.

Leaving me with the moose and without a word of explanation, he scurried off into the trees. I could only guess he planned to return with the men. Suddenly, I had no desire to meet with others of the People. I doubted they would accept me as the God of the Stone. I had no choice but to disappear until they had gone on their way. I hoped it would not be a long visit, as I was terribly unsure of my ability to survive alone without the skills of Hopelf. How long did it take to skin and butcher two moose?

I returned quickly, and I hoped silently, to the camp and gathered together the items I had carried to the mountain camp. After removing all traces of my existence, I walked into the woods away from the scene of the hunt. I could now hear the voices as they approached the kill. I climbed further up the hill trying to stay out of clear areas where I might be spotted, then after gathering water at yet another spring, I scurried up a large oak.

I have read that cornered or wounded animals always go up. I sensed my actions were much the same. I couldn't see the kill site or even hear the conversation clearly, only voices now and then. I settled in to wait.

Alone again. The day dragged on and on. I never left my tree. Hunger came and went, but not the heat of summer's dog day. Mid-afternoon saw the last of the water disappear. I could still hear the voices in the distance. I watched several white tail deer scurry off in the opposite direction after sniffing the wind. The smell of blood and man must have been strong. Late in the day, a gray squirrel became so accustomed to my presence he played up and down the length of the limb upon which I was perched. Boredom as it turned out became my greatest enemy.

As night approached, I listened to the voices coming closer. As they settled in at the camp, I could hear scraps of the conversation, and once thought I heard the name Tallilopka.

When dusk slid into true darkness, I left the tree and tried to slip silently up the hill. I was hungry and thirsty, but too afraid to return to the uncertainty of the camp. Even a visit to either of the springs would have been much too risky. In the darkness, I fell over vines and tree roots with most every step. Tree branches seemed to reach out for me. The forest sounds echoed in my ears. Finding myself under a large pine after one hard fall, I decided to stay put. I crawled under the low hanging branches, spread the two lightweight hides, and settled in for a night isolated from the protection of Hopelf's friendship. Not even the strongest of dreams could have eased my way that night.

Actually, I didn't dream, because I never really slept. I'd wondered all day if Hopelf had mentioned my appearance and now disappearance to the others. How had he explained the killing of two moose by a single hunter? He had not looked for me. I didn't kid myself into believing my skill at hiding would not be easily outdone by his skill at tracking. Did he believe Tallilopka had simply left on another of those famous journeys?

Now thoughts of home and safety came like constant companions. Mom was sure to be worried, since I had now been gone for three nights. How had she explained my absence, my disappearance? Had she called Dad? The police? Was there an

Amber Alert for me? She must have been worried sick. I imagined her crying. I wanted to hold her, to comfort her, and to be comforted. I needed a hug. Maybe Mom wasn't able to sleep either.

The darkness continued, the night crept on and on and on. I depended on the earlier dream to keep my spirits up, believing I would yet return to my natural time and place. Still, fear of the unknown controlled that night. Sounds in the obscurity of darkness surrounded me. Some I recognized as harmless, others were new to my ears. It was to those I listened quite intently while wanting only silence. Then the silence would become more frightening than the strange noises.

Morning came gently, catching me dozing from exhaustion. I watched the sun rise over the far mountains with a glorious red color. Red sky at morning, sailors take warning. I wondered if the saying would come true. All was quiet, except for the screech of a hawk overhead as he searched the forest floor for his next meal. Swooping lower and lower with each screaming turn, he positioned himself for a kill. Faster than my eyes could follow, he dove, then rose into the sky carrying a small rabbit in his beak. It struggled against its captor until death. I remembered my hunger. I returned to the tree to await the day's happenings.

There sat Hopelf on my branch. He gestured for me to remain quiet as I climbed. He presented me with roasted meat, presumably moose, and water, then left without a word being spoken. So he had known all along of my whereabouts. Somehow I was not surprised.

Soon I could hear the awakening of the camp. One of the men wandered in my direction to heed the call of nature. He was of medium build with straight black hair, bound back with a leather thong. His clothing appeared to be of the same style as Hopelf's with the exception of red dye on portions of his shirt. His pale gray chert gorget gleamed against his tan buckskin shirt. He walked with a limp, and I noticed his left leg did not seem to bend as he moved. I would try to remember to ask Hopelf about his injury.

I could see a trail some distance below me, and within the hour, I saw the heavily burdened men pass that way. Skinning and carving the two moose had taken an entire day. The last man's limp and all they carried confirmed them to be the hunters. I noticed one also carried several turkeys slung over his shoulder; another carried squirrels. It seemed their hunt had been successful in many ways.

Hopelf returned and beckoned me from the tree. I was happy to be on solid ground as my backside was sore from so much sitting.

"The hunters have returned to their camp with much of the meat. They will tell of my double kill before I have a chance to brag of it. I shared so much of the bounty they are sure to make it a good story. Tallilopka's name will not be mentioned except for his generosity. I took your absence to imply you did not want your presence known."

"That was my wish," I replied quite formally, for our easy acceptance of one another seemed strained.

"There is yet much meat and two hides to be carried to my camp. Will you help?"

"Yeah!" Something to do except sit and worry.

8
Storm

      Packing for the return trip proved much more tedious. The hunters had packed the butchered meat in the hides from their hunt. Hopelf, I soon discovered, had parted with a large share of the fresh moose. He made several bundles of various other items to be carried, antler tines, hoofs, and even pieces of gut which I now realized were the source of the many cords he used. In the camp, I discovered the hunters had left two turkeys in exchange for the moose meat. Hopelf had been presented with several eagle feathers. These expressed the hunter's pride over his kill. These he carefully packed in his knapsack.

We left the camp about noon. Again it was hot and with our added burden, walking proved hard work. Hiking up the mountain had pushed my legs and lungs to the limit and walking down seemed no easier. The load pushed me forward on the steep path. I felt as though I would tumble head over heels at any moment. It was like walking with brakes on.

We rested frequently. As I had not slept the night before, I often dozed while we rested. Hopelf also seemed tired.

Conversation proved virtually impossible since we had to walk single file and use all of our strength to carry the packs. It was strange to me that we saw few animals other than a squirrel on the path. Hopelf said they could smell the kill. I should have thought of that myself, duh!

We walked until dusk, yet I knew we had covered no more than one-third of the way to Hopelf's base camp. As we dropped the packs for the final time that day, each of us collapsed onto the soft grass of the clearing we had chosen for a camp.

"I am tired from watching over Greg during the night," Hopelf sighed.

"You watched last night while I was under the pine?"

"Yes, from a nearby tree, I didn't sleep while watching you not sleep," Hopelf answered very quietly, "for you seemed to need watching. Now we both need to eat."

Something seemed different in the way he spoke, but I couldn't quite put my finger on it. Was he suspicious, scared, nervous?

For the first time, we worked together to fix a meal, sharing responsibilities equally. Neither spoke of the work to be done, it was simply done by whomever was available. Hopelf carved off a chunk of the moose meat and left to fetch water while I started a fire. I also had time to begin building a lean-to because distant thunder threatened another night of rain. Hopelf managed to find some berries, and a strange root to add to our meal. He roasted the root under the coals of the fire. After peeling away the sooty exterior, the interior tasted very much like sweet potatoes.

We ate like starved African children under the dense canopy of trees and watched the lightning play across the sky. Later just as we had finished the shelter, the rains came. The winds whirled strongly, and branches blew from the older trees, as the saplings bent to touch the ground. Hail rained down and surrounded us on the ground like snowballs. It stung our bare skin as we left the shelter to pull the packs in with us. Now soaked, we began shaking in the chilled wind.

At first the lean-to sheltered us from the downpour. Yet as the storm continued to build, it failed to hold against the vicious whipping wind. Pieces flew off into the forest leaving us uncovered from the rain, hail, and wind. Hopelf and I pulled the packs closer against us, and by wrapping the lightweight hides over us and tucking the edges under the packs and some rocks, created a tight covering for ourselves against the elements.

The cold rain and harsh winds continued to build while lightening and the resulting thunder thrashed the forest around us. It grew incredibly stuffy in our makeshift tent, but our bodies' shared warmth finally allowed us to drift off into an uneasy sleep.

I awoke to quiet and dark. We had both pushed the hides askew during our slumber. The night air's chill bite had become intense. Shivering I struggled with the hides trying to cover us.

Hopelf awoke, probably because of my moving about. "Fire," he said.

Everything felt very wet around us, and of course, the camp fire had turned to wet ash. Rivulets of water ran across the camp toward the nearby stream. The forest's bounty of downed wood and limbs lay soaked all around us. Nothing remained dry.

I was sure Hopelf had lost his mind. A fire when everything was WET.

As the clouds broke and allowed the moon to shine through, Hopelf pulled a stone axe from his pack. He quickly proceeded to chop into an old fallen log lying nearby on the forest floor. When he reached the interior, he began pulling out hunks of the rotted inner material. Using this and his firestones, we soon achieved another fire. All of the firewood I had gathered earlier lay soaked, so the fire smoked heavily and burned weakly. Just as it began to get light, we were able to strip off our wet clothes and dry them by the fire. We wrapped ourselves in two of the slightly drier hides and huddled close by.

With the first few rays of sunlight, I surveyed the damage around us. Several old oaks and maples had fallen during the storm along with numerous branches and limbs. We could see one pine tree still smoking from a lightning strike. Its top stripped away with pieces of the bark hanging burned near the bottom, it stood black against the forest backdrop.

74

Hopelf went for water and returned with even more bad news. The path had changed to a muddy stream overnight. We needed to wait for at least one day of dry weather before continuing down the Long Mountain.

With nothing to do but wait, both of us curled up near the fire and slept, being exhausted after losing two nights of sleep. Late morning arrived before we had either the energy or desire to dress in our somewhat dry clothes or to feed ourselves. After a lazy meal of moose, we unpacked the remaining meat and began cutting it into long strips for drying. Hopelf had wanted to do this at his summer camp; however, if we waited, it would rot. I noticed it was beginning to smell even then. Actually, moose meat smelled gamey from the beginning.

This *little* project took several long exhausting hours. First, we built a drying rack of branches and cord so we could hang the meat. We were soon covered with sticky blood from the meat, making me glad we had stripped to only our pants before beginning. Thousands of deer flies were attracted by the smell and swarmed over us as we worked. Their bites were painful and caused welts all over my back, shoulders, and arms. Hopelf appeared as bothered by them as I was.

When the job was finished, we took turns fanning the flies from the drying meat while the other washed in a nearby stream. The cool water soothed the painful itching bites, but the stinging returned as soon as we dried.

Hopelf left me fanning the meat and went in search of a leaf he believed would bring relief. I hoped he was going to bring fresh meat for supper as I was famished. Also I didn't relish the thought of more moose since it has a strong flavor and is rather tough to chew. It made my jaws ache.

Now speaking of ache, my shoulders began to do the same. I fanned the flames to create more smoke and added a bit more of the wet wood. I realized when the smoke from the fire blew over the meat the flies left. So I quickly added even more wet logs to the fire to create even more smoke. By building another fire on the opposite side of the drying rack, I created a curtain of smoke around the meat. Then I stopped fanning. Good thing, for now I coughed from the smoke, and my eyes watered something fierce.

Sure Hopelf would be impressed with my discovery, I leaned casually against a tree and waited. He wasn't.

"Ah, Greg decided it would be easier to smoke

the meat, I agree. I should have added more wood to the fire before I left," he stated and began to pluck feathers from one of the turkeys.

So much for my brilliance. I had discovered, by accident, the ancient art of curing meat. (I think I'm getting better at writing sarcasm.)

"Did you find the leaf?" I asked.

"Yes, but first I must mash it with a stone and add hot water to create a paste as the Grandmothers have taught. It will take some time, but less if you will bring the water," he replied.

I returned with the water only to be sent back to the stream for several medium-sized smooth stones. Hopelf wanted smooth water worn stones about the size of a golf ball. Of course, he didn't describe them that way. He had never seen a golf ball.

Hopelf heated the stones in the fire and then dropped them into a large inverted turtle shell half filled with water. As the water began to boil, he added the smashed leaves. Soon it looked like mud, green mud. He allowed it to cool only slightly before applying it to my bites. The itching and stinging instantly stopped. So I covered him with the green gunk as well. It smelled of mint.

What a sight we must have been. Two boys dressed in filthy breeches (me in my cutoff jeans) covered with globs of green gook. Neither of us had combed our hair recently (I'm not sure how Hopelf combed his hair), and our feet and legs were speckled with mud from the previous night's storm. Days in the forest had caused scratches on various parts of our bodies. A sight to send a mother into shock. But neither of us cared.

Instead, with growling stomachs, we watched over a roasting turkey and fed the fires with damp logs to cure the meat. Happy and relaxed, I asked Hopelf to tell me some of his Grandmother's tales because I wanted to hear more of Tallilopka. He seemed eager to oblige.

9
Tallilopka

"Tallilopka was a grown man at his visit to the People of the Fast North Running River of the Mountains. These People live in the ways of the People of the Long River with the Long Mountain. They are of the Mother of All. They are our friends. They share our tongue, and we meet as brothers for the hunt.

"Now these People needed Tallilopka, as the eagles, and geese, and swans, and hawks had become so elusive the Birdhunters could not catch them. The glorious colored feathers were needed for the spring ceremonies of the People, the ceremonies to show reverence for the beginning of life from the Mother of All.

"The feathers they held looked worn and old. They did not please the Mother of All and her bounty became less and less with each coming year.

"Tallilopka arrived after hearing the long sorrowful speeches of the Grandmothers carried on the winds from the common camp. The speeches had foretold another year of death for many babies, both of the people and of the animals, if the Mother of All was not pleased with the offerings of the People. They spoke of the summer rains not falling from the heavens, and of the winter snows never ending. Years and years of poor hunts had caused sadness among the People. Women wailed for the dead babies buried to the Mother. The old and weak died during the harsh winters. The Grandmothers wanted the happiness of the People to return.

"It fell to the Birdhunters to make the Mother of All happy. The Birdhunters purified themselves in the cold waters of the Fast North Running River and awaited the morning of the hunt. As they waited in the darkness by the river, they talked of a successful and glorious hunt. Bait had been caught to trap the eagles and the hawks. As the birds of prey swooped down to retrieve the tethered rabbits, nets would be thrown over the magnificent birds. The Birdhunters would need to be swift.

"The ones prepared to catch geese and swans would swim into the river reeds and await the feeding birds, catching them by the legs and pulling them under until they drowned. Both methods were dangerous, since the birds of the Mother of All would fight their attackers to show their worthiness as sacrifice. Tough leather garments would protect the hunters, yet, some would be injured. The sacrifice was not too great. For a fruitful hunt would bring fame to each of these women.

"The Birdhunters would be the top choices as brides for the Mother of All would grant great favor on those who honored her with outstanding bravery. They would bear many children and live long lives. They would be Grandmothers of their People.

"With the breaking of the moon's light over the Earth, Tallilopka appeared before the Birdhunters. He was dressed in magnificent leathers and furs decorated with quills from the porcupine and feathers from blue and black jays, scarlet tanagers, indigo blue buntings, and the red of the cardinal. He carried only a rawhide cord, no spears, and no pack. His long hair was braided, a new idea for the People. He stood tall, over six feet, but was thin like one who labored in the ways of the People. The Birdhunters were speechless.

"Tallilopka called to the Birdhunters of the Water Birds, telling them to await his return. The Birdhunters of the Birds of Prey, he led to the steep cliffs of the mountains and positioned each with her bait for the coming of the dawn. Returning to the river more quickly than possible, Tallilopka led the women and girls into the cold dark waters only moments before the dawn and left them breathing through their reeds.

"With the orange glow of sunrise approaching over the mountains, each Birdhunter whispered her prayer, requesting of the Mother of All the cunning and strength for proper homage. Suddenly upon the morning winds, Tallilopka flew, calling to the birds of the water and the birds of prey. As he called, the Birdhunters who had remained speechless began issuing the same calls. From their throats and lips came the call of the birds they hunted.

"Leaving their nests, the birds responded in greater numbers than seen for many a year. Tallilopka continued to circle overhead, leading the birds to the reeds to feed and to the cliffs in search of prey. The Birdhunters became quiet as the hunt began. They took only the necessary number of birds for the celebration to the Mother, because each knew the secret of calling the birds to the kill. No longer would the mothers cry for lost children, or winter foods be scarce, as the Son of the Mother had given them another of his ideas.

"The Birdhunters saw Tallilopka soaring in wider and higher circles as the hunt continued, and with its end, he disappeared into the clouds of the sky. Only the Birdhunters had known of his presence. With their baskets and packs filled with birds of all types the hunt ended. Tallilopka flew out of sight into the setting sun. The People no longer needed him. The Birdhunters had an illustrious tale for the People, one spread from People to People as hunters met over the night fire. It is the tale of Tallilopka and the Birdhunters. That is why only Birdhunters braid their hair."

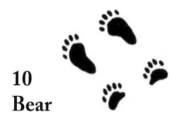

10
Bear

"Are there Birdhunters among your People?" I asked when he finished.

"Yes, we have Birdhunters, but they don't have the importance as with the People of the Fast North Running River. In our ceremonies, we honor the turtles and tortoises. We honor their hunters. With each People honoring different of the Mother of All's creatures, we remember her bountiful gifts to the People."

"Are there many groups of People?"

"There are many families of the Mother of All's People and many who do not worship her living in faraway lands over many mountains. They do not speak our tongue. We meet and trade and share the hunt. On occasions we marry with these people. It honors the Mother," Hopelf replied.

Much to my delight, he now began to carve the turkey. This gave me time to realize that if Mom could only use the information I was gathering in her reports, she would be famous. But I knew it was not possible, since all her information would have to be supported by a scientific base of knowledge. I thought of how Hopelf's family knew of distant tribes. How they traded, hunted, and lived peacefully with many different cultures, even ones that did not speak their language. They seemed to live together peacefully and for the benefit of all. Yet, Mom and other archaeologists had found evidence of what they took to be warfare among these peoples. I guess that was a story for another night.

As the day advanced into evening, the fires needed constant tending to keep the smoke swirling about the meat. Hopelf and I dragged into the camp all of the wet logs we could find. Neither of us wanted to be out searching the dark night for firewood. The wolves I had listened to for many nights were closer, attracted by the smell of the kill and today's butchering. Their howling seemed to ring in our ears, ever nearer with the falling of darkness. I'll admit I was afraid, even Hopelf seemed nervous. We went to the spring for a final time and watched dark forms moving in amongst the trees.

Over our meal of turkey, Hopelf explained how the wolves would stay away because of the fires, but we must be careful to keep them burning high. I added more wood just to be safe, you know—better safe than sorry. I volunteered for the first watch, knowing I couldn't sleep, while wondering how I would know when to wake Hopelf for his shift. Also, how could I sleep with all of that howling?

We pulled the now dry hides near the campfire and made beds upon piles of soft pine needles. Hopelf settled in leaving me staring into the fires and into the trees. I pulled the two spears closer yet.

I thought back to the days two years ago when I attended overnight camp for the first time. The days had been so full of new friends, swimming, archery, horseback riding, tennis, volleyball, you name it. So it was only at night that I missed my family. I would suddenly become very homesick and want to hug my mom and dad. Being alone that night brought back those same feelings. I had time to miss my own world, and I seriously began to wonder if I would ever return.

That was the fifth night. Perhaps I should have stayed at the point of my entrance into that previous time. I worried while feeding the fires and listening to the wolves. They did not approach any closer. Hopelf awoke on his own and took over the watch. I fell into a deep sleep and did not awake until the sun had risen high in the sky. Worrying makes me tired.

Hopelf packed the meat into the hides. It weighed much less dried, but we still had the massive hides to carry. We gobbled a breakfast of berries and doused the fires before leaving the camp. While the path was still muddy and walking difficult, we made good time, despite the numerous stops made to remove storm-fallen trees and branches from the path.

We reached the base of the mountain about dusk, finding a gentle stream near the path, and we unloaded our packs to feast on leftover turkey. I thought longingly of bread and lettuce and mayonnaise.

As I went for water Hopelf turned in the opposite direction and went off into the trees. I removed my footwear and soaked my aching feet in the cold stream while filling the water bag. An eagle circling overhead caught my attention, and I watched as it played amidst the currents of air.

I remained fascinated by its ability to effortlessly cruise the azure sky for endless moments, only to catch another updraft and soar even higher. Lying back against the bank, I observed it for a long while as it soared along in free flight, forgetting my duties and my companion.

Suddenly, abruptly, Hopelf's terrible, anguished scream of pain brought me crashing back to earth. Paradise had ended. Forgetting my shoes, and the water bag, I ran to the camp. Hopelf was not in sight. All was ominously quiet.

I called out. There was no answer. Unfocused, I darted into the forest where Hopelf had disappeared, calling his name over and over. I ran blindly, stumbling amongst the trees and shrubs, but was unable to locate him anywhere.

Then I came face to face with the bear. She was massive, her dark brown fur giving off a strong musky scent. She stood so close I could see berry juice on her snout. I froze perfectly still, I'm not sure whether it was from fright or wisdom. She slowly swung her head from side to side, drool running down in rivers from her mouth, and once rose on her hind legs. Yet, she did not attack.

I felt sick to my stomach with fear for myself and Hopelf. Her claws ran red with blood. That pain-filled scream vibrated still in my memory.

In the same breath, the same second, the bear and I began to move. I walked slowly backwards to the nearest tree. She turned and lumbered toward a rustling in the underbrush. Afraid it was Hopelf she was after, I rejoiced to see two cubs emerge and join their mother. Having learned my lesson about wandering alone in the forest unarmed and unprepared, I returned quickly to the camp for those two spears. I doubted my ability to use them, but knew I would no longer be afraid to try.

After retrieving my footgear and the water pouch, I gathered up one of the hide blankets. I knew Hopelf lay somewhere in the forest in serious trouble. That I might be his only hope was a scary, terrifying, grim thought.

I searched more carefully, calling his name louder and louder with each step, hoping he would answer. I also thought my yelling would scare away the bears. I found the berry patch again, and this time Hopelf's knapsack, dropped where he had been picking berries. His stone axe lay on the ground nearby.

I called out again several times before I heard his weak reply.

Alive!

The underbrush seemed disturbed all around making tracking impossible—as if I knew how to track. His cry wandered weakly through the trees. I remained unsure which direction to take. I called again, no response. I decided to circle the area about 10 feet out to try and pick up a trail.

Holding the spear at the ready with shaking hands and arms, I advanced into the thick berry and briar bushes. I had only walked a few feet into that tangled mess of thorns and undergrowth when I realized Hopelf could not have fled that way. So I returned to my point of origin and looked for a clearer path he might have taken in his flight.

Rewarded for my efforts, I soon discovered blood on a somewhat overgrown animal trail. The blood trail led me to Hopelf.

There he lay under a large pine, against the trunk as if he had taken refuge in its branches and had fallen. Now unconscious and bleeding badly from his left shoulder and leg, he looked dead. The shoulder wound ran across his back from the base of the neck to the armpit. It was bleeding heavily, but seemed to be only deep claw marks. The leg wound frightened me more. It encompassed the entire thigh with the major cut laying open the muscles all the way to the bone.

I'll admit, I was sick to my stomach.

Hopelf bled profusely, and I knew he would soon bleed to death without medical attention. Terrified, I realized his life lay in my hands. I began to panic, to scream for the dream to end, to plead for help.

Yet, I was alone.

No one would come to help. I was alone. All alone and scared.

Slowly, I came to my senses and remembered a beginning school class in first aid and tried to recollect the many techniques we had been taught. I treated Hopelf for shock by raising his feet and then tried to staunch the flow of blood from the leg wound. By pressing folded sections of the leather blanket hard against the wound, I was fairly successful. The bleeding slowed to a trickle.

Hopelf remained unconscious so I checked his breathing and his heartbeat. His breathing appeared shallow, but his heartbeat appeared strong.

I had hope.

Carefully, I wrapped him in the blanket and with great effort lifted him into my arms. He was heavier than I expected. I whispered a prayer for strength, to my God and to his Mother of All, and proceeded back to where we had left the packs.

I knew if I met up with the bear again, I was defenseless, since I had to leave the spears behind. I walked slowly and tried not to open the wound by moving him more than necessary. I had to stop once or twice and apply pressure. Hopelf now appeared very pale even with his darkly tanned skin.

Arriving back at our packs, I quickly make a bed of the hide blankets and laid Hopelf among them. I wanted to keep him warm. I gathered firewood and searched Hopelf's knapsack for the firestones. Unpracticed, it took me what seemed like hours to create even the tiniest flame. It seemed like years before I had a decent fire. I stopped several times to check his wounds, his breathing, and his heartbeat.

My scant training and years of listening to Mom fuss about bacteria had instilled in me the knowledge that infection would be his greatest enemy. So I boiled water and cut another of the hide blankets into strips for bandages. Unskilled with the stone knives, this proved difficult work even with his razor-like stone knives. I soaked some of the bandages in the water. I had to work fast to keep it boiling, adding the heated stones quickly and removing those that had cooled from the tortoise shell of water. Several times I had to go for more water.

Hopelf slept fitfully. I was glad, because next I needed to treat the wound. I began with his shoulder, carefully washing away the clotted and dried blood with the very warm strips. The scratches were not deep. One thing to be very thankful for. Next I treated the leg wound in the same manner, but the deep cut began bleeding again, causing Hopelf to moan with pain. So I wrapped it tightly to hold the wound closed, wondering if I should attempt sewing it closed. I didn't have the stomach or the tools for such an operation and decided to put off that decision until later. I could have tried a tourniquet, but that was dangerous if I got it too tight and cut off blood flow to his leg.

I gave Hopelf water, forcing it between his lips, while worrying about his pale face. Placing my hand behind his head to pour in the water, I discovered the lump on his head. He must have fallen from the tree or been pulled down by the bear. My worries mounted with each passing moment. As the day grew late, I attended to Hopelf and the tasks at hand, sick at heart and mind. Never, never had I felt so alone.

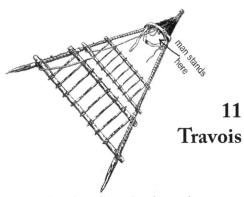

man stands here

11
Travois

With the approach of night, the hopelessness of our plight hit me with the same force the bear had used protecting her cubs. Tears of anguish and seeming defeat reddened my eyes and sobs broke forth with the intensity of all the fear I was feeling. I am not ashamed to admit I became afraid that Hopelf would die. How could I survive without his protection? I had come to depend on his know-how in all matters relating to survival—to life. This was a perilous predicament for us both.

I cried as I had that first night.

Only the sound of Hopelf screaming out in his sleep pulled me back to reality. As I held him against me to prevent him from thrashing about and reopening the wounds, I took upon myself total responsibility for our lives. If we were to survive, it depended entirely upon me.

For the first time in my life, without the aid of a can opener, I made soup. It wasn't tasty turkey soup, the kind with vegetables and noodles, but it tasted nourishing. I used only some of the turkey as the tortoise shell was too small to hold all of the meat. I fed Hopelf much of the cooled broth as the sun dropped behind Dans Mountain, leaving us to the uncertainty of darkness.

As I gathered more firewood for the night, I remembered the spears I had left behind. I picked up one of Hopelf's and quickly retrieved the others from under the pine. Ever watchful for the bears, I saw no wildlife at all until I approached the trail on the return trip. The raccoon did not hear my approach, and I was able to raise the spear and hurl it forward before he moved. With all honesty I must admit I did not actually hit the poor creature, nevertheless, in his panic, he ran right into the path of the wayward spear. My first kill—total ineptitude.

Returning to the camp, I found Hopelf awake, weak, and thirsty. I gave him more of the broth and some water before he slept. He did not complain of his pain. I think he wanted to appear brave.

I skinned the raccoon, doing a lousy job of it, butchered, and spitted the meat to roast over the fire. As I sat tending the fire, I made plans for the coming day. Dawn would come soon enough. I needed to be ready to transport Hopelf to his People. I knew I could locate one of the other boys to guide me to the camp. But I had Hopelf and the necessary supplies to transport. At least we had made it to the base of the mountain, leaving the steep slopes behind. The path here wove wider through the trees and except for the streams to be crossed it would be easier walking.

Before sleeping, I used the axe to chop three small trees. It amazed me how quickly the strong, man-made instrument cut into the meat of the tree. I stripped each of their branches and using the moose gut as cords. They were sticky with blood and other stuff and really gross. I created a rectangular travois frame. I found an awl, a bone needle without a hole, in Hopelf's knapsack and punched holes in one of the moose hides to use for a cover on the travois's frame. I thought again of sewing up Hopelf's wound but could not face that task.

I tied the hide on with strong vines, since I had used the remainder of the cord. I pleaded for it to hold. Only after building up the fire and packing away the roasted meat, did I retire for the night.

The moon already hung overhead leaving only a few hours until dawn. I knew I needed to rest, as tomorrow would be long on both body and mind. Listening to the night animals scurry among the trees and leaves, I watched the stars form the annual patterns overhead until I dropped off to sleep from sheer physical and mental exhaustion.

The night proved all too short.

I awoke early to find Hopelf thrashing about with a burning fever. He would not stay covered so I wrapped him in the remaining hide and bound it with a vine before placing him on the travois. He was not conscious, which I took for a bad sign. Not even stopping for breakfast before pushing forward on the trail, I found the pulling difficult, for the load was much too heavy. I removed most of the dried meat and the extra moose hide from the travois hoping we would both live to regret their loss.

The first stream necessitated the removal of Hopelf and the supplies from the travois. I had to carry each across separately and repack. I lost valuable time at each crossing and worried after Hopelf's condition. I forced more water between his parched lips. The fever raged and a check of the leg wound revealed swelling and some bleeding. Hoping it was the right kind of tree moss, I packed the wound and wrapped it with clean strips. I recalled the trick from some old John Wayne movie my father liked to watch. The moss supposedly contained penicillin or at least the movie said it did. As I pushed on, Hopelf quieted. The journey was hard on him—and me.

Just past noon I finally spotted the smoke of a fire. I had made the decision the night before to leave Hopelf on the trail if I saw evidence of another camp. Going to the camp alone through the woods would be faster, though the risk would be great for Hopelf. Not knowing the boy's name I called out Hopelf's name, as I ran. I ran on and on almost reaching the point of collapse when suddenly he stood before me on a slight trail visible only if you knew where to look.

"Hopelf is injured, needs help, please lead me to the camp," I babbled as he stood staring at my sudden appearance. As I fell to my knees to catch my breath, I got a glimpse of my appearance. The bloodstained clothing, a mixture of Indian dress and cutoffs, the splotches of green goop, the wet leather shoes, and scratched arms and legs made me appear as something out of a horror movie. Though this Indian boy had never experienced the big screen, the look on his face had that same stunned, horrified look.

Again I begged, "Please help me, a bear badly wounded my friend Hopelf. I need to take him to the People." He offered me water from his bag, and without looking back followed me through the forest to Hopelf.

Surprised he had listened without fear for himself, I remembered what Hopelf had said about their peaceful existence with the other tribes. This boy had nothing to fear. Neither did I. I should not have hidden from the men of Oma's family. Fear had blinded me. I swore not to let that happen again.

We found Hopelf restlessly lying on the travois.

Linka, as he was called, urged me to hurry, and we began pulling the travois. Working together, we managed it easier than it had been for me alone. Soon we achieved a slow, but steady trot and covered the miles quickly.

At the next stream as we rested briefly, Linka asked suspiciously, "Greg, where are your people, and how did you come to find Hopelf?"

I had already decided to ignore the God

of Stone routine and go for a simpler version so I replied, "Hopelf found me many days ago near his camp. We traveled up the mountain to kill moose. As we returned, a bear protecting her cubs attacked him while I had gone for water. How this happened is Hopelf's story to tell when he has recovered."

He received my answer with only a nod of belief, or perhaps disbelief. I couldn't tell and really didn't care, as long as he helped. While we drank from the stream, I again checked on Hopelf, he remained so pale, so very quiet I feared his death was imminent. Linka did not seem as worried, but urged us on with every step. I soon became exhausted and wanted to collapse into a nice soft bed and lie there until noon of next week.

Instead we pushed on covering mile after mile of the path along the bank of the Potomac. We stopped only for water and to cross the numerous streams winding their way to the river. Darkness fell, slowing us to a walk under the heavy canopy of trees.

I did not eat all day, except for a few berries, and though I had been hungry before, I only thought of Hopelf now. He awoke once, but did not recognize us as he begged for water. He drank thirstily, and I wished I could give him more of the nourishing turkey broth of the previous evening.

Only with the rising of the moon, did we push on faster into the night. I figure it was around two in the morning when we crossed the final stream. Linka gathered the supplies on his shoulders, and with me pulling the travois, we covered the final mile, exhausted, but oh so close to our destination.

Dawn broke over the hills on the far bank of the river as we reached the camp. Linka called out a name and our need for assistance as we neared the camp. What seemed like hundreds of people poured from the shelters. I recognized the man with the limp from the hunting party as I collapsed with relief upon the ground.

12
Hopelf's People

An entire week had passed since I traveled into that dimension. I awoke to the dim sunlight peeking into the bark-covered shelter where they had placed me. I had no idea of the time, but the noise of the busy camp made me believe it was midday at least. I started to rise and found my body to be uncooperative. I ached all over, from the bottom of my feet to the top of my head. It was then I noticed my feet were bandaged, and several cuts and blisters on my hands had been treated with a purple looking salve. My clothing, except for the cutoffs, had been removed and replaced with a clean leather shirt. I even seemed to have been bathed. Embarrassing. At least they hadn't removed my pants!

I eased myself into a sitting position to get a better look at my surroundings. Someone had constructed the shelter of interwoven branches in a kind of beehive shape. I remembered noticing the exterior covering of large overlapping pieces of bark on the previous night. Or morning, I wasn't sure which. There was a smoke hole in the ceiling over the cold black fire pit. No fire burned. The circular hut measured about seven feet across. Inside, besides for the pallet where I had been placed, lay one other. The remainder of the space was taken up by bags of all shapes and sizes plus numerous tortoise shells filled with various nuts, leaves, berries, etc. All of these appeared to have been dried. A water pouch hung from a branch across the doorway. As I reached for it, the same limping man from the hunting party blocked the doorway with his presence. I don't think he intended to prevent my escape, but rather to help me with the bag and attend to my needs. I was relieved to find it was he who had tended me in my sleep.

"Hopelf? Is he alive?" I asked frantically.

"Yes, Greg of the Then and Now People has saved our son who was on the Journey Alone. Our people are grateful for your courage and sacrifice in bringing Hopelf here. Your medicine is strong. He yet asks after his friend, Greg. Come, we will visit the Grandmother's home."

Then and Now People? What? Hopelf had told them that I just appeared? Did people that just appeared as if by magic not scare these people? Then and Now People, what the heck?

As we walked across the clearing, both of us limping, I realized Hopelf had not named me as the God of the Stone. No longer Tallilopka, I was glad to be only Greg. I also realized I was no longer afraid of everything about me, but confident enough to depend on myself and others. I knew I could not survive in this world alone.

We limped in unison across the center clearing of the village. Many of the People smiled and nodded, continuing their chores as we passed. Only the children approached, calling out to my new companion, Meela. He called to each by name and often was granted a smile or hug in return. I could tell he was loved by the People.

The Grandmother's larger hut sat slightly apart from the others. I knew this would be Oma, the head of this group. Linka had told me that this group was closer than any of the others. I expected an old graying woman with a cane to make her walking easier and was shocked to see a robust woman with only flecks of gray coloring her dark braided hair. She must have been a Birdhunter. Her simple leather clothing, covered in designs of what I could only assume were dyed porcupine quills fell to just below her knees.

Barefoot, she beckoned me forward, calling, "Greg, new son of the People, come talk with Hopelf, he calls for you." She grabbed me by the shoulders and hugged me with the intensity of a bear before allowing me to enter her home.

A fire burned in the central pit, giving off a strong yet pleasant aroma of hot herbs and roasting meat. Hopelf lay on a bed of many hides. Fresh bandages covered his leg, and he had recovered much of his natural coloring. Relief overwhelmed me. A young girl, perhaps eight or nine, fed him soup with small bits of the roasted meat and hot herb tea.

Meela entered the hut with me and checked Hopelf's condition. He seemed pleased and then excused himself to attend to a sick child. I realized he had to be the medicine man of the People.

"Eat, Greg. You must be famished. Linka told us of yesterday," she said, handing me a tortoise shell of rabbit meat and a cup of fresh cold water.

"Where is Linka?" I asked.

"He has returned to Hopelf's camp with several of the older men to secure his supplies and bring them to the Cray family. Linka will run ahead and tell Cray of Hopelf's injuries. His people remained here until only two days ago, their journey is not yet far. They are moving to their fall camp and will be worried not to find Hopelf awaiting their arrival."

Up until now the girl had not allowed Hopelf to speak except for a greeting as I arrived. I was anxious to speak with him privately, but did not want to insult the Grandmother. Hopelf suddenly brushed the girl aside, refusing any more food.

"Grandmother Oma, may Greg and I speak alone?" Nodding her head in response, she refilled my dish before shooing the girl from the shelter. After making sure our needs had been attended to, she smiled as one who understood the private concerns of boys and left us alone.

"Greg, later I will thank you for saving my life, but now I must explain. Since the night of the moose kill, I have known you are not Tallilopka. I know not of your people, but know you to be a brave and loyal friend. I know you are alone. You had great fear. If you wish to remain with the People you will be welcomed as my brother, and we would be greatly honored."

I thought his speech had been practiced and delivered with much feeling and forethought. But, I was still confused about those dang *Then and Now People*.

Emotion caused my voice to crack as I answered, "I will stay, but not forever, I must return to my people someday. I am proud to be your brother. I always begged my Mom and Dad for a brother or sister."

I didn't mention that lifesaving bit. That was embarrassing enough given that most of the time I had just stumbled upon the thing to do next.

"We must soon have a ceremony to honor your bravery. It will be fun, with lots of good things to eat. We will be the center of attention. Besides Tlin will be impressed," he rushed on without realizing my hesitation.

"Okay," I answered, causing a questioning look on Hopelf's face. Dang it, English slang sometimes slipped into my speech. Anyway, he took my meaning to be agreement. *If I couldn't be Tallilopka at least I could be a hero.* (More sarcasm!)

We finished the meal with Hopelf talking of the ceremonies and celebrations to come. He expected his family to arrive sometime the next day.

He was not sure if the entire group would return to the summer camp or if part of them would proceed to the fall camp to ensure enough food for the winter. He was excited about seeing his mother and father, but it was the mention of Tlin that brought a sparkle to his eyes. I wondered if our friendship would be as close when she arrived. I think I was jealous. I had never had a real girlfriend or even a friend that happened to be a girl.

Grandmother Oma reappeared at the hut entrance with a basket of berries and scolded us for not resting. I must admit I was still very tired. The young girl escorted me back to Meela's home as Oma tucked Hopelf into the hides for a nap. Meela assured me I could return at any time as Oma had invited us for the evening meal. I laid down, instantly closing my eyes.

I dozed, I thought back through the previous day's events and wondered how I had ever managed alone. Yet, I could not sleep soundly for something seemed to be needling me. I glanced about the room and realized the supplies and weapons I had carried down the mountain on the travois with Hopelf were missing. I knew these People would not steal, but I urgently needed to know the whereabouts of the knapsack which contained Mom's trowel, the projectile point, and the spears Hopelf had given me. I searched the hut for them with no success.

Rising to find Meela and ask for his assistance, I wondered at my intense concern over the trowel and the spear.

Meela sat tending a fire in the center of the camp. He scolded me for not resting before I even had time to explain my concern.

"Meela, I need the knapsack and the spear I was carrying yesterday. Do you know where they are?" I said, impolitely interrupting him.

"Greg, my hut is for medicine and never are the articles of everyday life stored with the healing gifts of the Mother. I will show you where those articles you returned with are stored if you will then rest."

Good. I nodded feeling much relieved.

13
Oma

I discovered Hopelf feeling a bit worse when I woke for the evening meal. I sat with him for a while, and we spoke of the upcoming ceremonies. He seemed exhausted, and I could tell he needed rest. I encouraged him to eat some of the thick broth Oma had made especially for him. Meela did not seem worried about Hopelf's condition and assured me it was a natural occurrence after any serious injury.

I watched as he changed the bandages on Hopelf's leg and gave him a cup of evil smelling tea to help him sleep. The leg wound appeared to be closing; however, I could tell some infection had set in. I knew that only time would tell how complete his recovery would be.

Meela used a mixture of herbs and tree moss to help fight the germs. I know he hadn't watched any John Wayne movies so he must have learned all this from his own experiences. Mom often said the early peoples traded medicinal herbs and passed their use from generation to generation.

It was approaching dark when I left Oma's shelter. The common area of the camp remained busy with families eating, children playing in the light of the many fires, and young people going about their chores. A noisy group, they called out to one another about the happenings of the day. It felt like listening to the six o'clock evening news with each person telling his own doings of the day to the others. Oma and Meela answered questions about Hopelf time after time, for the entire village seemed concerned about his welfare.

I tried to stay out of the center of things. I wanted to watch but not to answer any questions. Though Oma had prepared a meal for us, every other fire offered us the choice bits of theirs. I found myself presented with different kinds of meat, including bird, turkey, rabbit, and deer, along with berries of all kinds, nuts, and different vegetables. Some of these I could not identify. I tried to taste all of them, but found several not to my liking. These I tried to discard without being noticed.

One small boy, about two years old, took a liking to me and followed me wherever I went. He watched every move I made with his large, luminous, almost black eyes. I had noticed earlier the very young children wore no clothing during the warm days except for a gorget around their neck. As the evening became cooler, mothers brought forth long hide shirts for each to protect them from the evening's chill.

As the boy's mother slipped the shirt over his head, I took the opportunity to ask, "What is his name?"

"Hoop," she answered, "he is Tlin's brother and will soon be the brother of Hopelf whom you have saved."

Before I could reply, she was gone chasing a small girl with yet another shirt. So I called Hoop to me, and he responded with a large smile. He crawled into my lap to share the berries. I felt good to be so easily accepted into this family.

If I stayed, Hoop would also be my brother. *Finally, brothers! Won't Mom be surprised!*

It wasn't long until Hoop sat heavily asleep in my arms. The camp became quieter and quieter as families settled in. I handed Hoop off to his mother and followed Meela back to his shelter. Meela insisted on rebandaging my feet. I was horrified to see how raw and blistered they were. There had been little pain during the day so I was not prepared for the sight of my poor bloodied feet. Meela cleansed each and spread on a cooling salve that again smelled of mint. He insisted that I drink some of that evil smelling tea. It tasted just as bad as it looked and smelled.

I must have fallen asleep for the third time that day soon afterwards, since the next thing I remember was the smell of breakfast. I dressed quickly so as not to miss anything. I also wanted to check on Hopelf.

Hoop and Tlin's mother offered me tea—not the evil stuff—and stew for the morning meal. The tea needed sugar. I wanted to see about Hopelf, but Oma's shelter showed no sign of anyone being awake. Also, Meela had not been in his bed when I awoke. I sat with the meal and began to worry whether Hopelf had taken a turn for the worse during the night. I ate quietly and quickly while watching Oma's shelter.

The camp came to life around me, first slowly and then with more and more activity. The previous night's *news broadcasts* had revealed the People planned to move to their fall camp in two days' time. The move had now been postponed due to our arrival and Hopelf's injuries. Nevertheless, several of the men went ahead with a previously proposed bison hunt. The family still needed dried meat for the coming winter's food storehouse.

It seems they intended to track the bison, make the kill, butcher, and then dry the meat before joining their families at the fall camp. I wondered how the women would manage the children, the supplies, and the journey without the help of all of the stronger men. I guess I'm a bit of a male chauvinist—don't tell Mom.

The village contained many shelters but most stood empty as other family groups had departed for their fall and winter camps. Each family's shelters lay separated from the others by a small space with each group having its own common area for cooking and other activities. Oma's family occupied their area, but the other areas remained quiet and deserted. I wondered about the oldest Grandmother, who led them all. Which group did she live with? Hopelf had never mentioned her by name.

From a distant area of the camp, I heard the sounds of flint knapping. Someone sounded hard at work making or sharpening stone tools. I reminded myself to go and watch later. Having seen a modern flint knapper at a demonstration last year,

I was fascinated by their skill. I had even tried to flake a piece of chert. No go! It proved harder than it looked.

I knew from listening to Mom that Native Americans had heated the chert first so that it flaked more easily. One of her friends had misunderstood this and had tried knapping the still hot rocks. He had burns all over his hands. Of course, he had also tried heating the chert in his oven. Big, big mistake! One piece fractured into many smaller pieces that flew about in his oven breaking the glass door!

Hoop joined me as I finished my second bowl of stew. He brought me a small basket of berries. I had seen only a few baskets in the camp. This one, woven from grasses, appeared quite fragile. I filed that fact away for Mom. Archaeologists rarely find baskets as they don't survive buried in wet dirt for years. Once mom found the buried impression of a basket in what was once mud, just like the dinosaur prints in Texas.

As Hoop and I finished the berries, Meela stepped from Oma's hut, carrying several small tortoise shells. The young girl quickly followed and dumped old bandages into the nearest fire. Hoop followed right on my heels as I hobbled over to speak with Meela.

"Hi, Meela!" he yelled as we approached. These were the first words I had heard him utter. Meela lovingly scooped him up onto his shoulder after placing the bowls beside the fire.

"How is Hopelf?"

"The leg is better, and the fever has broken but he needs much rest. You may speak with him for a moment, but no longer."

"Me, too," Hoop begged. Meela nodded his head in agreement, and I grabbed the small boy from his shoulders and entered the hut.

A small fire burned near a sleeping Hopelf. Oma sat against the far side of the shelter working on a small soft hide. Again the shelter smelled of that foul herb tea. Hoop stared at Hopelf for a moment before whispering his name. Hopelf opened his eyes and smiled at us both.

"Hoop, will you take care of my friend for me today?" he asked in a still voice. Hoop only nodded and smiled. Hopelf assured me I would be in good hands before he dozed off. I was grateful now for two brothers. Before we left the hut, Oma asked after my injuries and if I had been fed. After assuring her as to both, I fled with Hoop.

The day flew by with Hoop first showing me his treasures. He had a pouch of toys, all handmade of course. These included a small wooden ball, a carved doll with no face but dressed in a leather shirt, much like his own, and a small spear with a very blunt point. We tossed the ball back and forth, though Hoop proved lousy at catching, and his aim was not much better. I figured that was why the spear was so blunt.

Later he and the other children waded in the river and brought up mussels for the evening meal. The older children caught fish with nets, showing surprising skill. No wonder Hopelf had laughed at my total lack of ability in this skill. Some of the older boys practiced throwing spears. They urged me to join though I was old enough to be considered a man by them. I proved to be much worse than I thought but quickly gained some measure of accuracy as we practiced. They laughed at my unpracticed technique and wondered aloud how I ever managed to feed myself. Yet, at the same time, they shared with me the secrets of their skill. I continued practicing until my arm and shoulder began to ache from so much unaccustomed activity.

Lunch turned out to be an each-man-for-himself type deal. We helped ourselves to roasting meat, stew, nuts and berries, and settled down to eat. My thoughts turned to home. I craved a hamburger with pickles, onions, ketchup, and mustard with a large milkshake. I missed Mom and worried about her constantly as I knew she must be worrying about me. At least I hope she was worried.

Hoop pulled me back from my daydreaming by telling me to eat. He seemed to be in a hurry to go somewhere or do something. I was rescued by Meela who insisted I rest and give my feet a chance to heal. We sat by the fire and talked while Meela sorted and bundled up his medicines for the coming journey. Hoop soon fell fast asleep at my side.

"Meela, how did you injure your leg?" I asked tenatively.

"It is not an injury; I was born with a bad leg. It is from the Mother," he replied in a very matter of fact tone.

"Why did you become the medicine man?" I asked hoping he would not feel my questions were invasions of his privacy.

"Oh, now that is a long story..." Meela sat quietly, thinking. After a while, he replied, "but we have time. You see, at the time of my Journey Alone I had not been promised to any young girl. None had caught my fancy and few wanted a man who limped. Yet, it was still necessary to become a man by proving I had learned the lessons taught by the mothers and fathers. I knew this would be difficult, as my leg makes many labors extremely strenuous because I move so slowly. As I left the camp for my first summer, many of the People lay ill. The winter had been hard, and supplies ran low. I traveled to the far end of the valley in order to hunt without taking food needed by the families. Many of the hunters could not travel far in search of food as they had only just recovered from the fever.

Each of the boys that summer left fresh game and berries at the fires during the night, because the People could not hunt enough to feed themselves. After several weeks, I met a very old man from another group of the Mother's People. He traveled alone searching for roots and herbs to restock his medicine bag. He stayed with me for a time and taught me what he knew. I had a knack for being able to identify the different plants and remember their uses and healing properties. I learned much from the old man in return for providing him with food and assistance in his search.

When I returned at the coloring of the leaves, many of the People had recovered their good health, but several of the old and very young lay still quite ill. I used the knowledge the old man had given me to prepare a tea. Slowly, most of the people recovered their strength. It was then the People made me an apprentice to the family's current medicine woman. She taught me her skills, and I took her place when she died. Even now I look for someone to take over after me. It is the way of the People."

After pausing for a moment, Meela asked something I could not explain, "How did Greg learn his healing powers? I saw the moss on Hopelf's leg and knew you had some knowledge, like many of the Then and Now People."

I had no answer that would make sense, so I just didn't answer. Instead I pondered on those *Then and Now People.*

Meela did not push for an answer.

14
Family

Dusk settled in around us with a light mist. The cooking fires sputtered as many of the People took shelter under large bark-covered canopies erected in the common area. I joined Meela and sat helping to sort some nuts in the dim firelight when Hopelf's family arrived. Only his immediate family had returned to the summer camp, his mother and father, a brother and his wife, and a younger sister. Of course, Tlin came with them. Many of the People rushed to aid them in lowering and unpacking the large bundles each carried.

Tlin's mother rushed to embrace the daughter she was soon to give in marriage to my friend.

Several of the elders escorted them to an empty shelter in Oma's area which I had been told always stood ready for guests. Hopelf's mother seemed harried and anxious to see her son. To this end, Meela stepped forward and escorted them quickly to Oma's hut. I remained under the canopy.

Oma had only appeared once during the afternoon to receive gifts of food from different members of the group. Having lost her husband many years before, the family provided for her wellbeing. The young girl, often seen about, fetched water and firewood for her, but otherwise the hut had remained quiet. If it had not been for Meela assuring me all was well with my friend, I might have worried myself to death. Now again I could only wait.

I felt left out and more than a bit apprehensive.

Hopelf's younger sister, Mova, soon appeared in the doorway, the first to leave the hut. She met with Meela who gave her food and water. The two of them seemed to be great friends despite the immense difference in their ages. They quickly fell into a conversation that involved much movement of hands and nodding.

Hopelf's brother, sister-in-law, and Tlin made their appearance next. Each called back to Hopelf a good wish as they bent to leave the hut. They made their way to the guest house and quietly began to unpack in preparation for the coming night. I noticed the boys who had taught me to throw the spear carrying up firewood. Several young women prepared a meal for Hopelf's family. No one had given orders for these tasks. They were just done. Tlin's mother and Hoop rushed over to help. Hoop, of course, seemed more bother than help, and Tlin grabbed him up in a hug to prevent any damage due to his overgenerous and enthusiastic helpfulness.

Then I was summoned.

"Greg!" Oma called out in a demanding voice.

I must have jumped a mile high. Crooking her finger, she beckoned me forward to her home and escorted me in the doorway. I felt as scared as with my earlier encounter with the mother bear. I remember shaking and feared my voice would crack if I dared to speak. I wanted to turn and run but could only stand paralyzed with fear. I'm not sure why.

I need not have worried though, since smiles all around soon greeted my entrance. Hopelf's father, a tall muscular man, rose encompassing me in his massive arms with a hug that threatened to squeeze the life out of me. His mother kissed my nose, the top of my head, and hugged me almost as hard, tears all the while spilling down her pleasant face. Hopelf tried to introduce us all. Oma finally stepped in and completed the introductions. His mother's name was Lehu, and his father was Hoef.

Over and over they thanked me for saving their son. I kept protesting and trying to tell of what Hopelf had done for me, but I don't believe they heard a word I said. Meela arrived and saved the day by insisting Hopelf had endured enough excitement, and we all should rest and eat. As they left the hut, I stayed for a moment to speak with Hopelf alone.

"Who did you tell them I am?"

"I told them you are my friend, and that we met at my camp, you were alone and without a family or people. No more needs to be said for you have proven yourself to be a man who is a friend to the People. My people welcome you for as long as you wish to remain. Now go and eat and sneak me some meat if you can. I am sick of broth and weak tea."

Laughing as I went, I rose to leave, promising to return with the meat if at all possible. "Man" rang in my ears—he called me a *man*. Wow.

125

"Greg," he called as I ducked out the door, "I am happy you are my friend and not the God of the Stone."

"Me too!"

Meela waited outside the door. "Someday you must explain why Hopelf thought you were Tallilopka," he teased. "But don't worry, I will keep the secret you two young men share."

I could only nod and smile as we joined the others. The whole camp now gathered under the large canopies. Most had finished their meal but the late arrivals were only beginning. I sat by Hopelf's father. Several people brought me more food than I ever could have eaten. I hid some away for Hopelf hoping Meela had not heard that part of the conversation. Oma moved about the group like a worrying dog with new pups. She moved constantly making sure everyone was settled, well fed, and content.

The children played in and out of the rain causing mothers to scold. A new baby cried in the background. Several constantly tended large fires lit the scene. The younger boys fed small branches into each fire as needed. I wished for a camera or my phone to capture the moment. Even now I can still vividly recall that evening. *Special.*

The evening news began with Hopelf's family telling of Linka's arrival and their journey back to the common camp. They also brought news of bison and elk in the meadow near their autumn camp. This seemed to foretell of a hard winter and plans for additional hunts quickly formed among the remaining men. News from the common camp was repeated quickly for it had been a quiet day. One of the boys tried telling of my lack of spear throwing skill, but was quickly hushed by his mother. I guess they did not want to insult me. So I told the story myself causing great laughter. I told you I like to talk.

As the evening progressed, families began to depart for their homes. Mothers rounded up the small children, many of whom lay already asleep in the arms of the older members of the group. The evening developed a definite chill to the air, so hides had been passed about to ward off the cold.

Hopelf's family discussed with others the upcoming ceremonies to be held in one day's time. The preparations required much cooperation. Oma handed out duties right and left. Hopelf's brother, who seemed to be about seventeen, received the responsibility for hunting deer for the feast. He had only one day to accomplish this feat, but seemed totally unconcerned. Tlin, Hopelf's mother, and his sister-in-law accepted duties as well. Hoef it seemed would coordinate preparing the special area used for such ceremonies.

"What can I do to help?" I asked.

There was dead silence before Oma answered, "You are being honored for your courage and are not expected or allowed to help. You may keep Hopelf company tomorrow. With all of the activity, it would not be wise for you to practice with the spear as you might injure yourself and ruin our celebration," she answered with a laugh. The joke seemed to relieve the tension caused by my stupid question.

I kept forgetting that I was the *hero* they were honoring.

"Then I will see to him now for he must be lonely," I said excusing myself. This gave me a chance to slip him the meat I had saved.

I had not seen Tlin leave the group, but there she was sitting with Hopelf when I peeked inside to see if he was asleep. They were talking quietly. I did not want to interrupt so I turned to leave. I was feeling left out, and I'll admit it, just a bit jealous.

"Greg, please do not go because of me. Come and join us," she whispered from the door.

I turned to find her smiling and beckoning me inside. No wonder Hopelf was looking forward to the end of the summer. She was a knock out. She reminded me of one of the girls at the pool. She stood only about five feet tall, and had the most beautiful dark long hair which she wore loose about her shoulders. Her amber eyes lit up her face when she smiled, something she did every time she looked at Hopelf. Some guys have all the luck.

I offered Hopelf the food I had smuggled in. Tlin protested, while Hopelf claimed to being starved to death, making Tlin change her mind. We sat for a long time joking, talking, and just enjoying each other. Tlin had news from the summer to share with Hopelf.

Many of her stories told of funny things that had happened in the common camp. Though I did not know the individuals about which she spoke, I could relate them to people I knew in my time and world. Some of her funniest stories were of a young couple that quarreled constantly. She told of how they would yell and throw things at each other all day causing the whole camp to wonder if they would kill each other. Then some little thing would happen, and they would make up only to begin the fight again within the hour. The Grandmothers had given up trying to reconcile their differences and now only stood and laughed with the others.

She told of births, three girls and a boy, and deaths among the very old, of great hunts the men had made, and of the boy interested in his sister, Mova. She told how Mova remained more curious about the plants and herbs used in medicine than in boys. Finally Oma came and chased us out, scolding us each for keeping Hopelf awake and for feeding him. It seems nothing escaped her notice.

I returned to Meela's hut and found him fast asleep. I tried to do the same. It was not easy.

Finally, I drifted off thinking of how I might return to my dimension while wondering how I could bear to leave this place. Somehow the answer seemed closer than before, and yet further away.

**15
Life**

Morning dawned cool. The hint of coming rain hung about the camp even after the fog lifted. Around the camp, hardwood leaves had just begun to show their fall colors. School would be starting soon. I wondered if I would be listed as absent or just dropped from the roll book completely. I dressed quickly after bathing in the river. Meela had borrowed some clothes for me so I washed the cutoffs and my underwear. The leather clothing was soft, but it felt strange to only have my pants tied on with a cord instead of securely fastened with a zipper or buttons. I worried all day about losing them. The soft leather chafed a bit in all those private places. No underwear! Dad calls that "going commando."

After breakfast, I visited Hopelf. Meela sat dressing his wound, and I could tell it looked much better. The claw marks on Hopelf's shoulder had already formed scabs. I figured they would leave a permanent scar for all to see and be reminded of a mother bear's fury when protecting her cubs. Hopelf had been lucky though. Had he been alone, he would have surely died. We talked until Lehu arrived with his breakfast. She brought his favorite stew. Mothers are all alike, first they baby you until you are well and then fuss at you for getting sick or injured. Hopelf's mother began already to nag him about being more careful.

I kept trying to leave without being noticed when she spoke directly to me, "Greg, you are to keep Hopelf company for the day, but first you are needed by Hoef. He will meet you at the central fire pit."

Some escape. I get away from his mother only to be sent to his father. I hoped he wouldn't hug me again as my ribs still ached from the last squeezing.

"Ah! Greg, please come with me," Hoef said as I approached. Then he led me away to the area where the older men were creating the numerous stone tools needed by the people of the camp. While most of the individuals could chip out rough tools, the really fine sharp ones required greater skill.

The process for their manufacture was complex and had been refined and passed down from generation to generation. I also knew it changed as they adapted their hunts to different game animals.

Because the flakes of stone were sharp and easily able to cut, the knapping area sat a distance from the camp, located in a small forest clearing to the east. A fire constantly burned in order to fire-treat the stones. There, wearing leather aprons and using a collection of chipping tools, such as antler tines, bone tools, and wood, the craftsmen created knives, scrapers, projectile points, and ceremonial items. They worked hour after hour during the best light of the day. Most were men but a few women labored among the most skilled.

The knappers treated each stone, which had been carried from the riverside and hillside quarries as well as traded from different tribes, with dignity. Each piece was seen as a gift from Tallilopka. Special pieces, those deemed most beautiful, became ceremonial items. Other craftsmen used softer steatite or soapstone to carve the gorgets worn by all the tribal members, even small children. I had noticed earlier that each member of Oma's clan wore the same design.

Hopelf's gorget appeared similar, yet different. I think these marked the members of each clan.

Upon our arrival a small, withered old man who was instructing several of the younger boys and girls on his craft rose to meet me. He spoke firmly with great emphasis. Like me, he used his hands to demonstrate his words.

"Objects of stone which are to have great value when given as a gift must be chosen by the future owner. Tallilopka will then guide my hand as I create the finished token. Therefore, *you* must choose from these stones the one which calls to you. Hoef has commissioned me to make an item for you. Come, choose. Let the stones call to you."

He stepped back to show me a pile of black, gray, even white chert, quartz, and beautiful red and yellow jaspers. Each quarry stone was about the size of a softball with rough edges where it had been broken from the mountain of its formation. Each looked distinct. But the red jasper with its darker, almost black veins and shiny surface drew my attention immediately. I am not certain it called to me, however, I reached out and held it in my hand to allow the sharp morning light to play on its surfaces. Its beauty astounded me.

The old man nodded in agreement with my choice.

"Yes, it is suitable. Now, go! I have work to do," he said, hustling us out of his space.

I did not ask what was to be made of the stone. I knew I would find out soon enough.

Returning to Oma's hut proved an accomplishment in itself. Everyone bustled about in anticipation of the coming event. Even the smallest of children helped. Hoop acted busy collecting firewood and berries. Other members of the large family packed in preparation for the coming move. Tlin spoke as she hurried by, quickly hiding something under her arm. Again I didn't ask, but silently ducked into Oma's hut to spend the day with Hopelf.

We spent the day talking, laughing, eating, and playing several games involving betting that were loved by his People. I had nothing to bet except the ring and chain I still wore about my neck, my cutoffs, and Mom's trowel. None of which I wanted to risk losing. So we played for fun, betting piles of small pebbles we used like poker chips. I turned out to be lousy at most of the games. Hopelf kept slipping me more of his stones to keep the game going.

Late in the afternoon, I helped Hopelf move outside to sit against the front of the hut. There he could watch the preparations. In the distance, the sounds of chipping stone could still be heard even as the sun began to dip behind Dans Mountain causing the trees to blaze with the sunlight reflecting their newly formed autumn colors. Tlin and the other girls had gone to the river to bathe. Their joyful noises could also be heard. Amazing how much they sounded just like the girls at the pool.

Hoop joined us and immediately tried to sit on Hopelf's lap. I rescued my friend from certain pain at the last possible moment. Hoop stuck out his bottom lip in a pout, but quickly regained his normal happy disposition when allowed to play with the pebbles from our game. Having napped during the early afternoon, Hopelf now expressed intense hunger. We watched the many fires and smelled the fantastic aromas of roasting meat while wishing we could hurry the process.

Suddenly, Hopelf's brother caused a commotion by arriving with a large ten point buck and news he had also killed a bison only a mile or so from the camp. The older boys returned with him to the kill site to butcher the meat before returning to camp later that evening or early the next morning. Seems we would enjoy quite a feast on the coming day.

Meela and Mova had spent the day packing his medicine bags and helping with a sick child. No doubt Mova would be chosen as his apprentice during the coming year. Hopelf said she was already respected among his direct family for her healing arts. Their medicine woman had died during the previous winter while still young, leaving their group without medical help during the harshest parts of the winter. If someone became extremely ill, a runner had to be sent to the nearest camp to ask for help. It seems Meela would need to train yet another person to take over for him when it became necessary.

Tlin joined us for only a moment, whispering something to Hopelf before she left to help serve the common meal. The camp had worked together during the day at all tasks including the evening meal. Each hut had provided provisions and all of the women had teamed together in its preparations. It was like wilderness stew, a little bit of this and a little bit of that.

Just at dusk the rain began to fall in earnest. Meela helped me carry Hopelf back inside. He expressed his disappointment at not being allowed to sit under the canopy in the evening hours, but Meela insisted he save his strength for the coming day.

The day ended with the sounds of falling rain upon fallen leaves. The bark roofs covered with spruce branches kept the huts fairly dry, and each remained warm from a small fire on that dark, wet night. Wood smoke hung heavy in the damp air. I went to bed early, surrounded by heavy furs to keep me warm. I remember clearly one dream. My mother stood calling to me, from the woodland clearing where I had entered this time. She kept saying, "Greg, don't forget my trowel."

I awoke to hear myself repeating those words over and over again. Now fully awake, I determined my mother had totally lost her mind over my disappearance. I mean, I had been gone for ten days and all she could think of was her dang trowel. It was either that or she hadn't missed me at all. No, no, that couldn't be it. She had lost it, really lost it, that was the only conceivable answer. Yet, I reminded myself to retrieve the trowel the first thing the next morning, then fell asleep again only to dream of the girls at the pool. At least that dream made sense.

16
Preparations

You know how Harry Potter didn't feel like or want to be the "chosen one?" Well, I didn't feel like a hero when I awoke any more than I had any other morning of my life. I don't feel like a hero now. Nevertheless, that day, a whole tribe of people treated *me* like a hero.

The sunlight brought a clear, cool autumn day. At dawn, Meela awakened me by insisting I bathe in the Potomac. Man was that water ever cold! Since they didn't use soap, I was given some leaves to use instead. They did create a bit of suds when wet and rubbed against the skin. I didn't stay in the water long enough to find out if they would make real bubbles. I dried quickly and turned to dress only to find my clothes gone. Now here was I, stark naked, wet, freezing to death, and only feet from a camp full of women.

Meela rescued me from being discovered or freezing by arriving at the river bank with clean, new leather garments. I had intended on dressing in my own denim cutoffs, but when I was told these had been made especially for me, I couldn't very well refuse. They fit well. The shirt was undecorated but the leather lay soft and supple against my skin. The pants hung long, and I was given a pair of leather shoes like the ones Hopelf had lent me earlier. The previous pair was worn out after all the walking I had done. The boots were designed to fit over the lower pants leg and tied off just below the knee.

Except for the color of my hair and eyes, I now looked like one of the People. I had even tanned a bit during the past week. Mom always made me wear sun screen. Boy would she worry about skin cancer when she saw me. Nah, she would still be going on about that trowel!

When we returned to the camp, everyone sat casually eating breakfast. I asked permission to join Hopelf but this was denied. Oma's look when she said "no" was enough to discourage me from asking why. I ate quickly so as to watch the bison being prepared for roasting. Hopelf's brother and the other young men had already returned, and some women hurried about preparing for the feast.

The men brought the bison haunches to camp intact and prepared them for roasting. A large fire pit was constructed while the younger children gathered stones for the lining. The older children gathered firewood. Since so many people had lived there during the summer months, wood proved scarce. As the children roamed in search of the valuable necessity, the older men and boys followed them with spears for protection. Several women rubbed the raw meat with a coarse salt and stuck pieces of herbs into pockets they made in the meat. A large fire burned in the pit but it was a couple of hours before the coals grew hot enough to hang the now spitted huge haunches of meat. Many members of the group took turns tending the fire and helped to turn the spit when needed.

Others started making stews from the inner organs of the bison. I hate liver and determined that I would just turn those pieces away politely when the time came. Some young women roasted almost a whole deer in a buried fire pit. They positioned heated coals in a shallow pit which they covered quickly with large smoothed river stones. The meat came next surrounded by different plants and vegetables. More stones covered the meat. They built and tended a fire on top of that small mound. This acted like an oven leaving the meat tender and juicy. It seems the People preferred this method for deer as the pit lay ready for use at the edge of the camp. With so many people working, they accomplished the whole process quite quickly.

Finally, others stripped some of the meat and dried it to be used on the coming journey to their next camp. I avoided this area because I knew it would draw those horrible biting flies. No more green goop for me.

Tlin complimented me on the fit of my clothes. I figured out she had helped Lehu with the sewing. The leather had been prepared earlier from kills Hopelf had made during the previous winter. I had several people to thank for my new garments.

I remembered the trowel at that point and decided to go to the storage hut and retrieve it. While there, I found the two spears Hopelf had given me. Also, the knapsacks contained some very raunchy meat which no one had thought to throw away. Man, did it smell up the place. I took some time to clean out each knapsack, at a distance from camp, and left them outside to air out. I hoped this would help alleviate the foul smell. Hoef noticed my activities and offered a pleasant-smelling leaf to place in each to help remove the rancid odor. It smelled a little like turkey dressing—probably sage.

"I should have thought of this earlier, then this would not have been necessary," I explained.

"Meela told me you were exhausted when you returned with Hopelf. It is no wonder you forgot to care for the belongings of my son. Likewise Hopelf told me you had nothing of your own except for the strange knife you held. I also know you had little knowledge of how to survive. I will not ask why, or question you about your past. However, I suspect you are from the Then and Now people. When you have a need for knowledge, come to me. I will give it gladly as any father would for his son," Hoef replied.

"Thank you, there is much I need to learn, and much your son has already taught me," I replied. I wanted to speak with him further, but he was called away to help at the site where the ceremony would be held. I had already been told not to go there until Meela said it was time.

Noon arrived before I finished the task. In so doing, I found the eagle feathers the hunters had presented to Hopelf. These I carefully smoothed out and rubbed with the pleasant smelling leaf.

Sticking the trowel in the top of my boot—no pockets in Indian clothes—I returned to camp to find Hopelf hobbling on Meela's arm from the direction of the river. I guess they tried to freeze him to death as well. Hopelf proved to be stronger than he looked that day I first saw him. I also knew he was older than my first impression. I had asked his age earlier and found out he had seen 14 winters.

Hopelf came back dressed in new clothing. He and Meela stopped at the central fire where Tlin helped with the preparations. Joining the group, I handed Hopelf the feathers while explaining my previous hours' work.

"Hopelf, why did you not tell that you had been so honored?" questioned Meela. "We must celebrate your achievement tonight also."

"Do you feel up to telling of the hunt? Did you do it alone or did Greg help? When did it happen?" Tlin asked, running the questions together in her excitement. Isn't that just like a girl? Ask a question and not even give you time to answer before asking the next one.

"Tlin, slow down and I will explain," Hopelf replied.

"I did not tell you of the hunt and the feathers because I forgot until Greg arrived with the feathers. I will tell the story tonight at the feast. Greg, did you bring back the hides and the meat also? How did you manage?"

I answered quickly before he had time to ask another question. "Yes and no, I was only able to return with one of the hides, the other and some of the dried meat I had to leave behind. I intended to return for it, but I forgot. I'm sorry."

"I understand you had a lot to carry! We will speak of it later when Tlin is not present," he replied making her angry at being left out. As she stomped off in a huff, Hopelf laughed, "She will lose her anger when she hears the hides were meant as a wedding gift."

"You can still give her one of them. But... I made several small holes in it. I hope it won't matter. I think some of the men and boys retrieved the others from your camp. You should ask."

"After hearing tonight of how you saved my life, I'm sure she will forgive us both. Now let's eat."

Hopelf ate heartily. I became convinced he would recover. He complained of some pain in his leg when he tried to stand but the wound was healing nicely. We shared the meal with Hoop, who always seemed to know the right time to show up and share everyone's food.

He kept us laughing throughout lunch with his imitations of a hawk that circled overhead. The camp began to emit a terrific smell of roasting meat. I had of course had bison burgers and bison pot roast, but now I would have my chance at fresh, 1,000 B.C. bison. Somehow it seemed different.

Hopelf and I played the betting game again while watching the activities around us. Then Hopelf and Hoop napped in the afternoon sun. I just sat and enjoyed the quiet.

17
Ceremony

Late afternoon brought on a sudden flurry of activity. Women and men alike carried tortoise shells of food and large hunks of the roasted meat, which had been carved and placed on bark and soapstone platters, to the ceremonial site. I saw the smoke of new fires from the rise above the camp.

Meela and several of the young men arrived to escort Hopelf and myself. They carried Hopelf the mile or more on a well-worn path. The site centered on a knoll about 300 yards from the banks of the river, surrounded by fragrant spruce trees. I remember clearly seeing Dans Mountain, as well as the Potomac winding off in each direction. The sun, having long ago reached its zenith, neared the top of the mountains which are now part of West Virginia. All the hardwood leaves blazed bright with color, yellows, golds, and reds, leaving only the numerous evergreens to provide the forest with some continuing green.

Fires burned in a circle at the clearing edge surrounding a large fire pit located in the middle. The People surrounded the central fire, all dressed in clothes like the ones I had been presented with, even the children and women. Only Meela's had the red coloring which I took to denote his position as medicine man. Oma's hides shined white, so white they must have come from albino animals. She even wore a white fur resembling squirrel about her shoulders. She looked very impressive.

However, my attention quickly turned to another woman dressed all in white. This old, very thin woman with wrinkled brown skin stood in the center, commanding everyone's attention with her soft yet firm voice. She stood very straight as she spoke to her People.

"People, make welcome Greg and Hopelf, whom we gather to honor."

Meela gestured us forward, but I remained reluctant until Hopelf urged me on. Several men escorted us to seats by the fire, surrounded by Hopelf's family and the Grandmothers.

The feast began. I ate until I was stuffed and afraid the cord holding up my pants would break. It felt like Thanksgiving when you try to eat everything, knowing you will suffer later for eating so much, but you still eat two pieces of pie.

I loved the bison, rich and juicy. Hopelf told me it was tender because it was a young bison. I also had deer, and stew, and even vegetables. After all this came a mixture of nuts and maple syrup. The People saved this rich sugary treat for special occasions. But, even the stew hinted at the addition of maple syrup.

Everyone drank a hot tea flavored with more maple syrup or just plain cold water. Dark had fallen by the time we finished. Hoop's stomach actually seemed to grow larger from all he ate. I feared he really would explode. Now having seen many movies about Indians, I expected the ceremony to be accompanied by drum beats and dancing. Wrong, wrong, wrong!

It began with the oldest Grandmother speaking to her people of the heros of the past.

Heros of hunts long past when mastodons ruled the forests, heroes of famines who saved the People, heros of the water, even a hero that saved the People from what must have been a tornado. She spoke of many, many deeds. As she spoke, the children chanted refrains of her stories. They all knew and loved the stories.

Then Oma added the story of a more recent hero who saved many, but not all, during an earthquake when the roof of a rock shelter fractured and fell. Well over an hour passed when only the Grandmothers spoke, telling their stories. Occasionally a young child would speak out, only to be hushed, or a baby would whimper before being put to a breast to feed, all else stayed quiet and listened. I remember being mesmerized.

Then Oma said my name. She beckoned Hopelf forward to tell our tale to the People. Hopelf spoke, beginning quietly, of our meeting, of how I appeared from nowhere. He spoke of mistaking me for Tallilopka. I expected laughter, but none came. His story went on. He told of fishing, of the trip up the mountain, and even my sore feet. But the climax of his tale proved to be my greatest embarrassment, the moose hunt. I wanted to hide when he called out "shoo, moosey, moosey." But, they did not laugh.

Alas, they didn't understand English, good thing for me!

Here the hunters interrupted and told of the magnificent kill Hopelf had made. Meela spoke of knowing of my existence at that point. I wondered how he knew. Now Hopelf regained the attention of all. His family presented him with great honors, since he had proven himself to be a first class hunter. He would now be allowed to hunt bison with the older men. Those once smelly eagle feathers they tied on the same cord which held his gorget. They looked spectacular lying against his tanned chest. Tlin beamed with pride.

Soon, the People urged Hopelf to continue with his story. He recounted the events of the storm with extraordinary detail. Finally, he told of the bear's attack. I listened intently for even I had never heard this part.

"Greg and I were tired from hauling the meat and hides down the mountain trail. As Greg went for water, I decided to go for berries and nuts I knew to be only a short distance from the stream. I failed to pick up my spear and remembered it only after reaching the berry bushes. I surveyed the area and saw no bears. Since I only intended to pick a few berries, I did not feel it necessary to return for the weapon. A mistake. I had not even begun to pick berries when the two cubs darted from the undergrowth. Busy chasing each other, playing, they did not even notice me. But the mother did. I did not even see her before she leaped on my back.

With my shoulder bleeding and in great pain, I managed to hit her once with my bag. The stone axe must have hit her fairly hard, because she roared in pain and backed off. I tried to run to a tree but as we all know, bear is faster than man. She reached me quickly and tore at my leg with her great teeth. Only the scream of one of the cubs drew her away. That playful scream saved my life. I still hear my screams as I climbed the tree fearful of her return. I remember only the pain of Greg tending my wounds and later Meela doing the same. The rest is Greg's story."

Forced to tell the rest of the story, and somewhat embarrassed, I told it quickly and without describing my own turmoil and fears about the events as they occurred. I mentioned Linka, giving him great credit for his help in reaching the camp. But my humility proved not totally successful, as Meela insisted on telling of my exhaustion and torn hands and feet. He also told of how I had urged the men to retrieve Hopelf's stores, meat, and hides, knowing of their importance to him. I became more embarrassed with each passing moment.

Next Oma's turned to speak. She talked of the importance of life, the gift of the Mother of All. The People listened earnestly to the story they had heard so many times before. The story of how the Mother had sacrificed all of herself to create the land, sky, water, everything upon it, and in it, giving her life to create the People. It was a powerful story of giving. Life reigned all important, not only because it was the gift, but also because each person depended on the others for survival.

The ceremony progressed now to a different stage. Those closest to Hopelf thanked me for my efforts on his behalf. I felt grateful for their words, but wanted to stop the whole event and tell of my fear.

As if he had read my mind, Hoef finished by saying, "Though Greg seems new to the skills of the People and unsure of our land, he carried on, hiding his fears as we all must do, in order to properly honor the Mother. We give him our respect for he is a man worthy of the Mother."

Lehu handed him an object, as he beckoned me forward. As he hung the shining jasper gorget around my neck, he said, "This is in friendship and brotherhood Greg, my son. I give you this amulet as a symbol of the protection of the Mother of All and

Tallilopka, the God of the Stone. You are now of the People."

Everyone joined in what I can only call a *group hug* during the next few moments. Then, and only then, they gave me the chance to reply. Holding back tears of joy I spoke, "I came here from a faraway place, lost and full of fear, now I have a family and friends. I hope only to be worthy of your trust. I have nothing to give to you in return for your gifts, for this I am sorry."

"No, Greg, you have given us a life, the most important gift of all," replied Oma.

The celebration continued with even more storytelling and feasting. There was no wild dancing to primitive drum beats. Instead, the People shared their pleasure over the happy event by recalling the glorious moments of their history, of the times they remembered and the times out of mind. I sat with Hopelf and Tlin. As the younger children fell asleep, they were placed beside their parents who continued to enjoy the stories.

The older men acted out several of the humorous tales, causing much laughter at their antics. As the moon rose and the time became very late, the group broke up to return to the camp for a short rest before dawn. Tlin walked with Hopelf, who was being carried by Hoef, and me on the return to the camp. I now had time to thank her for the clothing I wore.

"It was too little a gift in exchange for Hopelf," she answered quietly, "someday we have agreed to name a son after you."

"Yes," laughed Hopelf, "but we will call him Greg not Tallilopka."

Somehow the teasing didn't even affect me. We joked back and forth along the trail. I teased Hopelf about becoming a father and caused Tlin to redden with embarrassment. Then she teased me about not even having a girlfriend at my age. She made me feel silly.

Hoef promised to ask Oma to find me a wife. If she was as pretty as Tlin, I would have been very happy, but I wasn't sure I was ready for marriage.

As we reached the camp and parted for the night, I thought back over the previous two weeks. I knew I had changed. I no longer feared everything new. I don't think I was even a geek anymore. I realized I had become capable of dealing with the events of each new day. I had two sets of friends and family who would always support me no matter what.

Yet, I was not content. I did not belong in this era. I had to return. Somehow I knew it would be soon. The hardest part would be saying goodbye. I prepared for bed while thinking of Mom and Dad, I hoped they would be pleased with the new Greg. I know I was.

18
Moving

A hawk screaming outside woke me early the next morning. The camp remained quiet, since the celebration had continued late into the night. The People were tired and needed rest for the journey they would soon begin. I left the hut and went to the river, as I had now become accustomed to the cold water swims. I swam across the river and back before leaving the water and dressing. I looked up, surprised, to find Hopelf watching me.

"Greg, Oma's family will move to their autumn camp today. I must return with my parents and Tlin to my people. I hope you will join us."

"I will begin the journey with you, but I cannot promise to remain. I feel a need to return to my people just as you do. I cannot explain why, even I do not understand… I continued trying to explain.

"I do not ask for reasons, Greg. Now come, let us eat before we begin the long walk," Hopelf answered picking up a sturdy pole he used as a cane. I could tell walking any distance would be painful for him.

"How will you travel? You cannot walk any great distances yet."

"My family will pull me on a travois, as you did. I did not want it to be necessary, but as you can see, I am not yet strong."

We quietly returned to camp only to find everyone awake and busy. Each consumed a hot meal of leftovers as the families packed the remainder of their meager belongings. I noticed several travois-type contraptions being loaded. They did not carry much from camp to camp, but this would be easier than the heavy packs Hopelf's family had arrived carrying. Mothers dressed the children for the journey, each wearing the leather boots and a long shirt. Many already carried small pouches which Hopelf said contained the food they would consume during the walk.

Meela stood ready, and I arrived to find the hut empty except for my clothing. I had dressed in my cutoffs and the leather shirt and boots. The other clothing I stuffed into the knapsack Hopelf had lent me. I picked up Mom's trowel and started to add it to the mess in the pouch but decided at the last moment to place it in my back pocket. I enjoyed having pockets again.

Hoef had brought over the two spears from the storage hut. I knew they were mine now and might come in handy, so I gathered them and the pouch and proceeded to join Meela for leftover, cold bison.

Oma soon gathered the adults around her and spoke of the day's journey. They set a distance to travel and an order of march. She and Meela led and set the pace. The women with small children followed next, then the older children and women pulling the travois fell into line. The few men left in camp came last. They helped with any problems and ranged out in search of fresh game for the evening meal.

The other Grandmother appeared from a hut, set a bit away toward some trees. Several young men came to her, carrying packs and spears. They all departed very quietly in a different direction. I never even learned her name.

Hopelf's family planned to travel only a short distance with the group before turning off to join their family group. I decided to travel with them. They doused the fires and left the camp in an orderly fashion so it could be reused the following year. One hut contained items the families could not or did not wish to take with them. It also contained dried meat, nuts, and tubers. It would be there when they returned unless someone traveling through had need of it during the winter.

Oma called us to the front when the journey began. "There will be no time to talk once we begin walking, so I will wish you a good trip now. Greg, we will be happy to welcome you to our camp, but I know you have chosen to join Hopelf for the winter. It is a wise decision. Take care."

Then she called to her people and set off on the trail along the Potomac with the family following noisily along. Tlin's mother said a tearful goodbye to her daughter. They would not see each other again until spring. By then, she would be Hopelf's wife, for they would be married after the last bison hunt before the first snow of winter. Hoop begged to go along with his sister, but was comforted instead by Mova, Hopelf's sister. Her decision to stay with Meela for the winter and learn more about his healing craft excited her family and her clan. The young boys would not be as happy, as the medicine woman or man rarely married.

I last saw each, Meela and Mova, walking along pulling his travois with Hoop riding happily on Meela's shoulders. We traveled several miles before the two parties split. Oma's group turned inward away from the river toward the mountain. Their fall camp lay at its base, from there they would later travel to a rock shelter on the far side of the mountain crest, arriving shortly before the first snow if they were lucky. The journey's last part would be the hardest, since they would be carrying and hauling large loads of meat and other foods for the coming winter. Game became scarce on the mountain during the snows.

Hopelf's family continued on the river path. Each of us took turns pulling the travois. We walked single file without speaking, giving my mind time to concentrate on what was to be. I had been here for two weeks now. Time enough for my picture to appear on missing children posters. I felt ready to go home.

We walked through lunch, eating the tough dried meat and berries we carried in our packs. Lifting both ends of the travois, we easily crossed the streams which had caused so many problems on my previous journey along this same path. The day became warm, and I stripped off my shirt. Hoef soon did the same. The air was still without a hint of a breeze. It would surely rain later in the day.

Finally at what I figured was about one o'clock, I realized we were near the spot of Mom's site. I felt pulled by some mysterious force to return. Hopelf sensed my feelings.

"Father, Greg and I wish to walk to my old camp. It is not far. We will join you on down the path." Hoef protested but Hopelf insisted. He let us go.

I turned to say a goodbye before I became fully aware of what I was doing. I knew I would not see them again. It hurt. They were now much more than friends. They were my family.

Instead I said nothing, for words could not convey my feelings. Turning away and holding back tears, I helped Hopelf as we walked into the forest from the trail. We did not speak. I carried my spears, but had left the pouch on the travois.

We soon reached the small clearing. The remains of the fire where we had shared our first meal lay evident to the past. "You are leaving. You are not Tallilopka, but you must be a god, for I know you will not simply walk back to your people.

You did not walk to the Long Valley. You simply appeared."

"Yes, Hopelf, I am going home. I am not a god, simply a man like you. I told you I could not explain." I reached up to remove the chain holding the ring my father had given me, but my actions were stopped by Hopelf's look of dismay.

"No, never remove your amulet. My People believe it controls life."

"But Hopelf, I wish to give you this as a gift. I have nothing else to offer. It will be a token of our friendship and brotherhood," I replied.

He only shook his head no in response.

"How will you explain to Hoef and Lehu and the others when I do not return?"

"I will simply say you have gone. Then over the winter fires when we tell our tales, I will have the newest and the best story to fill the hearts and minds of our People. The story of Greg will be repeated until a time out of mind."

"Here, take one of the spears. You don't want to meet up with another bear and be unable to defend yourself," I teased, handing Hopelf the extra spear he had given me so many days before.

We stood in silence, Hopelf leaning on his cane and holding the spear. I held only the spear with the beautiful quartz point. There was so much to say. But no words seemed to work. Instead, we touched hands and said goodbye.

For an instant, I wondered how I was to return to my time, to home. I couldn't click my heels together and whisper "there's no place like home, there's no place like home." I didn't have any ruby slippers.

As Hopelf turned to leave, a rustling in the forest caught my attention. Suddenly a rabbit jumped into the clearing. Without stopping to think, I raised the spear and threw it with all the skill and technique I had so recently learned. My aim held true. Holding the jasper amulet tightly in my hand, I thanked Tallilopka.

As I reached down to retrieve the rabbit, I saw Mom's trowel shining against the forest leaves where it must have fallen from my pocket. I picked up both the rabbit and the trowel with one motion, then removed the spear point from the rabbit. The shaft fell away to the ground. Hopelf started to speak as I handed him the rabbit, but when I did, the point and the trowel touched.

He was gone.

19
Home

I was back. Everything remained just as I had left it, the screens and tripods, the pool across the street, even my sandwich just lying there at the edge of the square. I turned to find Mom being helped to her feet by one of the girls from the pool. Mom looked terrible and was holding her head.

"Where have you been? Didn't you know your mother was hit on the head by one of the canopy poles? How could you leave her here like that? Boys!"

Girls are all the same, no matter what the era. I started to explain but Mom stopped me.

166

"It's okay. Greg just went to the van for our drinks," Mom said, covering for me. "Thank you for your help, but I feel much better now."

"Oh, okay, well…I just came over from the pool because, well because, I've been curious about your work," the girl replied quietly. "May I come back tomorrow and help out?" She smiled at both of us.

"Of course," Mom answered. We waited until the girl had gone before speaking to each other. Then I handed Mom her trowel and sat down beside her. I noticed the leather boots were gone and reached to feel for the gorget. It was still around my neck. Mom smiled as she examined it.

"Greg, for a moment I had a glimpse of you in a forest clearing, holding a spear, a rabbit, and my trowel. There was another boy there. This came from there didn't it?"

"Yeah, it's a long story."

I didn't tell her the story right there and then. Strangely enough, she didn't ask. Instead we closed down the site for the day and sent the volunteers home. We went home and then talked all afternoon. Mom listened. I talked. I do that you know.

I became suspicious when she believed me so readily. Finally, Mom admitted to having been there herself, you know in *a time out of mind*. It seems Mom is one of those Then and Now People, just like me. Even weirder, I had been there before as a young child. That's how I could understand their language. Mom knew it too. She admitted to having traveled back in time on several occasions. What a shock! Just when you think you know someone. I wonder if Dad knows?

Anyway, I still have the gorget. I never take it off, though I replaced the cord with a stronger one, a bit more modern and less smelly than moose gut. Mom put her trowel back in with her equipment. She still uses it for features. The quartz projectile point is on display in a small archeological museum near here. I go by and look at it every now and then. I spend a lot of time doing volunteer work there. I help with the collections and give guided tours.

As for that girl, Rose, well, she returned the next day, and the next, and every day thereafter. We work at the site in the afternoons after school. We do homework together. She's really smart and learns quickly. She plays Minecraft. She even works at the museum and comes to the archeological society meetings. I spend a lot of time with her. I talk, sometimes too much. She listens.

She has the most beautiful smile and dark amber eyes just like Tlin's. Maybe someday I'll let her read this, or maybe I'll just introduce her to a Time Out of Mind.

Glossary of Archaeological Terms:

archaeology - the scientific study of how people lived in the past based on artifacts found in the soil

archaeological artifact - an object left in the soil by people who lived in the past, such as a pottery sherd, coin, or projectile point

arrow head - the tip of an arrow, called a projectile point by archaeologists

feature - a stain left in the soil by past activities of man, such as a red stain left by a fire

gorget - a decorative stone, shell, or metal ornament usually worn around the neck, often carved

Native American - another name for an American Indian

prehistoric - existing in a period before written history

projectile point - arrow or spear point, usually made of stone. Example shown is made of milky quartz. Size ranges from about 1" in length up to about 8".

screen - a wooden box with a heavy screen mesh bottom used to sift soil to find artifacts

travois - a triangular frame used to pull a heavy load, usually by a man, horse or dog

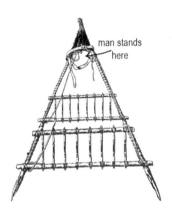

man stands here

tripod - a stand holding a screen for sifting dirt for artifacts

trowel - a triangular-pointed blade hand tool used by archaeologists

About the Author

C.M. Huddleston is a Registered Professional Archaeologist with more than 25 years experience. C.M. Huddleston worked at the Cresaptown excavations in the mid 1980s.

All of the archaeological terms and techniques described in this book are accurate. The Native American tales told by Hopelf are based on real Native American legends from several tribes.

Learn more about Greg and his coming adventures in time travel at www.cmhuddleston. com.

Moose illustration by Pearson Scott Foresman on Wikimedia Commons. Cover by Interpreting Times Past, LLC.